BUTTONS AND GRACE

PENELOPE SKY

Hartwick Publishing

Buttons and Grace

Contents

Chapter 1

CANE

I sat on the couch beside Adelina with my arm draped over her shoulders. We were both watching TV, but I knew neither one of us was really thinking about the content on the screen. I risked my neck to save her life, and when I told her what she meant to me, she didn't feel the same way back.

It fucking hurt.

I had been certain she felt the same way, thought I felt it in every kiss she gave me. She had just returned from a gruesome captivity, and she didn't refrain from touching me. She wanted me all over her, my lips sealed to her mouth.

But that didn't mean anything.

Now here we were—in painful silence.

My phone rang, and Pearl's name was on the screen. I

hadn't spoken to her since the raid, so I assumed it was important. I took the call and pressed the phone to my ear. "Hey, I—"

"Crow has been captured." She spoke a million miles an hour. "Tristan took him from the house, and now they're heading east. Get him, Cane. Now!"

My reflexes were quick, and I was on my feet instantly. I darted for the pistol sitting on the counter and shoved it into the back of my jeans. I grabbed the bulletproof vest still sitting out. "I'm moving."

"Hurry!"

I hung up and strapped on the vest as I headed out the door. My pulse was thudding in my ears, and I could barely hear my surroundings. The sounds from the TV disappeared and Adelina said something, but I couldn't make it out. I grabbed the machine gun from the closet and bolted out the front door.

"Cane!" Adelina ran after me. "What's going on?"

"Stay inside." I didn't turn back to her as I ran to the car. "I have to go. I can't talk." I cranked the engine and sped off, heading toward Cane's house on the other side of the fields. I made a call to Bran on the way, telling him to gather up everyone he could and head to my tracker point. When that was done, I pulled up Crow's location on the center screen.

It was still working.

Thank fucking god.

I hit the gas harder and sped nearly a hundred miles an

hour down the empty roads. It was almost midnight, so no one was on the streets, thankfully. Now I knew Tristan was alive, and this time, I wouldn't let him slip away. He would regret taking my brother when I beat him to death with the end of my shotgun.

I followed the tracker and tried to gain on them, but they were driving furiously just the way I was. They were heading east, which told me they intended to stay in Italy. There was no chance they were taking Crow on a plane unless they had a private one. But even then, that seemed unlikely.

Bran spoke over my phone system in the car. "We're ten minutes behind you. What's the plan?"

"Haul ass. Tristan is alive, and he has Crow. They must be returning to their base, and they have no idea we're tracking—" The dot with Crow's position suddenly disappeared. The map was completely blank. The vicinity where he had been was now empty.

"Cane?" Bran said. "You cut out."

I refreshed the page and pulled the map back up on the screen.

His coordinate was gone. "Fuck…"

"What?"

I slammed my hand so hard against the steering wheel I nearly broke the bones. "They found the fucking tracker. Jesus Christ." Tristan must have run a scanner across his body the second they were on the road. They obviously found the transmitter and cut it out.

Pearl must have just seen the same thing.

"Shit," Bran said. "What do we do?"

I didn't have an answer. I never panicked in stressful situations, even if they were a matter of life and death. But this was my brother, and losing him scared me far more than losing my own life. The whole reason he was captured was because of me. I should be the one tied up in the back of that car—not him.

I couldn't handle the guilt.

I couldn't face Pearl.

I couldn't face myself.

"Cane?" Bran repeated.

I kept driving even though I no longer had a destination. "They were headed east. If they were planning on flying out, they would have headed to Florence. They must be going to Rome or somewhere in that vicinity."

"What's the description? What kind of cars are we looking for?"

"I...I don't know." I had no idea what happened at the estate. Pearl made it sound like they snatched Crow and left. There wasn't a single witness to help me.

"Cane, I need something more than that."

"I know," I hissed. "I don't have anything, Bran. I just know we need to find Crow as soon as possible—" My phone started to beep as someone called me on the other line. It was an unknown number, and due to the situation I was in, I thought it would be stupid to ignore it. "Hold on, Bran." I hit the button and switched over. "Cane." My tone immediately changed, turning defensive in preparation for whatever would happen next.

"Hope you're enjoying my whore as much as I did."

The voice was unmistakable, and it didn't take me longer than a nanosecond to figure out who it was.

"And I'm enjoying your brother. Not in the same way, of course." He added a sarcastic chuckle, enjoying his revenge thoroughly. I hadn't said a word, but he knew I was panicking in my silence. "Now that the tracker is gone, you'll have a very difficult time finding us. If I were you, I'd save the gas money."

Fuck. Fuck. Fuck.

I wasn't letting my brother die. I wasn't letting him suffer when this was all my fault. I wasn't letting Pearl become a widow and single mother. Not gonna happen.

"So, let me save you some time. Give me what I want, and I'll hand him over."

I knew he was going to ask for Adelina. I didn't want to give her up, even if she didn't love me. She was an innocent woman who deserved to be free. But Crow was my brother, my blood. I was a dick to him, but that didn't change how much he meant to me. I loved him from the bottom of my heart. It made me sick to my stomach, but I'd have to hand over Adelina to get him back. He was family. I wouldn't turn my back on him and Pearl like that. Adelina would understand.

"Give me Pearl."

My hand gripped the steering wheel tighter, and I

swerved slightly as I drove down the street. It was dark in the countryside, and I could see the lights from Florence up ahead. Pearl was the last person I expected him to ask for.

"I'll give you twenty-four hours to think it over. But you better give me the answer I want to hear—or he dies."

"Why do you want her?" I demanded. "I'm the one who killed your men. I'm the one who stole your woman. Let me take his place, and you can get the revenge that you deserve. Beat me, torture me, and kill me."

He chuckled. "As tempting as that sounds, my idea is much better. I know how you Barsettis work. It'll hurt you much more knowing all the horrible things I'm doing to him than anything I could physically do to you."

Fuck.

"But I want Pearl so I can hurt both of you. Ever since I laid eyes on her, I've thought of all the things I want to do to her. That flawless skin, those bright eyes… I can't wait to snuff the life out of her just the way I did to Adelina."

I squeezed the steering wheel so tightly my knuckles turned white.

"Give her to me, and Crow walks free. I'm a merciful man. I'll allow you to save your brother—for a price."

Chapter 2

CROW

I was in a warehouse in Rome. Even with my tracker ripped out of my arm, it was a foolish place to put me. Cane would have been hot on my trail when the connection was severed, so he must have confirmed I was staying in Italy. My brother was an idiot, but when it came to the important stuff, he was observant.

Ironically, I was just thirty minutes away from Bones's old base. Tristan probably chose it because it was so close to home. Cane would never expect me to be sitting in his backyard. Once the tracker was gone, I knew this would become a more difficult situation. It would be much harder for me to escape. Even harder to be rescued.

But Cane was smart, and so were the men working for us. Cane wouldn't sleep until he found me.

But Button...she was sobbing at this very minute.

She was more scared than she'd ever been in her life.

If she lost me, she would lose part of herself.

I couldn't think about it too much because it would break my heart. I had to get out of here for her. I had to get out of here for the little Barsetti growing inside her. I wouldn't deny my child the security of having a powerful man around to protect them. If I had a son, I would teach him how to love by the way I loved his mother. If I had a daughter, I would teach her what to expect from a man who wanted to be her suitor—if he was brave enough to shake my hand.

But in the event I didn't make it out of there alive, I knew Button would be okay.

That woman was strong.

She would be devastated, but she would carry on without me. She would have my fortune and my brother to protect her. She would still raise my son to be a man, and my daughter to be stronger than I ever was.

She could do it.

But I didn't want to make her.

I had to get out of here.

I was in a small warehouse by myself. The concrete was damp from a leak in one of the pipes. That told me I was inside an older compound, something that would be located on the outskirts. A few chains hung from the ceiling, telling me this place was initially used for heavy shipments. That meant we were near a road so large trucks could easily access the area. I probably wouldn't get the opportunity to speak to Cane, but if I did, I needed to give him as much information as possible.

My right eye was swollen shut, and the right side of my jaw was broken. Tristan had stabbed me through the forearm, careful to miss an artery but his blade penetrated enough for me to bleed all over the floor and make me weak. A lot of my ribs were broken. The pulse in my temple wouldn't stop pounding. He gave me a good beating, seeking revenge for all the men I killed.

I didn't make a single noise the entire time.

I'd known what was coming. I'd known how to handle it. I wouldn't give him the satisfaction of causing me true pain. The only thing that could really hurt me was my wife. And she was far away and protected by my best men.

Tristan had nothing against me.

The door opened, and a shadow appeared as Tristan's silhouette emerged. His boots thudded against the hard concrete as he approached me with guards on either side of the door watching him in silence. Each had a gun on his hip.

My hands were tied behind my back. My ankles were locked together in chains. There was no way I could get out of this by myself, not unless I found a decent tool to get me free. I watched Tristan walk toward me and finally saw his face come into view.

His lip was curled in a permanent sneer, his long nose was hooked like a claw. His bushy eyebrows needed to be maintained, and his eyes were the color of oil spots from a broken-down car. I pitied Adelina for having to fuck a man so ugly.

Tristan stopped in front of me, his arms hanging by his sides. He had a gun, but he didn't draw it. "You look like shit, Crow."

I spit a stream of blood off to the side. He'd punched me in the mouth a few times. "Still look better than you."

His eyes narrowed in assault. "You're either very brave or very stupid."

"They're the same thing, if you ask me." I wouldn't be intimidated by this man or any man. To show fear was a death sentence. Pleading and begging wouldn't save my life. It would only cost me my dignity just before my life ended.

Tristan grabbed a chair from the side and placed it in front of me. He took a seat, like a long conversation was about to happen. "Have you enjoyed your stay with us?"

"It's not a five-star resort, but it's good enough."

The more playful I was, the more it irritated him. He knew he would never be as brave as me if he were in the same situation. He tried to exert his power over me, but he could never be successful when I wouldn't allow it. "I spoke to your brother."

"How's he doing?" I projected an aura of calm indifference, but that was all just an act. I had to figure out a way to get back to my wife—my pregnant wife.

"He's been better," he said. "Didn't say much."

"Probably because he's busy screwing your former prisoner."

Tristan's eyes narrowed again, and this time, it looked like he might hit me. Maybe he would lose his temper and just shoot me. But if he did, he would have no leverage to get Adelina back. That must be what this is about. He was pissed she was taken, and he was using me as a hostage to get her back. I had no idea if Cane would make the switch or not. On the one hand, I was his brother, and he would do anything to save me. On the other, she was the woman he loved. If I were given the choice, it would be hard to make the decision. "The only way you're getting out of here is by a trade."

My suspicions were correct.

"Tell me where your wife is, and I'll let you go."

I did my best to hide my reaction, but I could barely control it. He'd asked about Pearl earlier, but I thought that was because he planned to kidnap both of us. But it appeared that he was still after her. "I don't see how she's relevant. She had nothing to do with Adelina's kidnapping."

"You're right. She had nothing to do with that. But ever since I laid eyes on those gorgeous tits and long legs, I've wanted to fuck her just the way you do, Crow."

All the blood drained from my heart as it was pumped to my extremities. My muscles got a shot of adrenaline, and they automatically twitched in preparation for battle. If I weren't restrained right now, I'd kill Tristan with my bare hands. I'd claw his eyes out before I ripped apart the rest of him, tearing off his limbs and fingers.

Remaining stoic in that moment was the hardest thing I'd ever had to do. I couldn't rise to his anger. I had to keep playing it cool because getting me angry was exactly what he wanted. Defending my wife's honor wasn't the priority right now. All Button wanted was for me to come back to her. She couldn't care less about Tristan's sinister intentions.

"You're going to tell me where she is. Once I have her, I'll let you go. Seems like a fair punishment for the way you both screwed me over. You get your freedom, and you can imagine what your wife is doing every hour of the day while she's chained to my bed." His eyes bored into mine, full of vengeful hostility.

I didn't blink. "I'm not going to lie and say I don't know where she is. I know exactly where she is. But there's nothing you can do to make me hand her over. You can cut off every single limb piece by piece until there's nothing left or I bleed out and die. You can torture me in whatever way gets you off. I still won't say a damn word. If you don't believe me, call my bluff. Break out the saws and drills and kill me slowly." I was the one who remained tied up and beaten, but I never lost my confidence or authority. Tristan was at my mercy because he was trying to break in to an unbreakable vault. There was no amount of money or weapons that could get him any closer to his goal. I'd gladly die before I let a man go near the woman I loved.

Tristan studied my gaze like the very words I spoke were written across my face. He didn't smile or frown, soaking up my message like a sponge. He rose from his chair and pushed it aside. "I told Cane that's the only trade I'm willing to make. So, in either case, one of you is going to crack. I'm just not sure who it's going to be."

Cane knew exactly what I would want in this situation. Even if he handed over Pearl, got me out of there, and then we teamed up to steal her back, I wouldn't want that. I didn't want a man to even touch my wife's hand, no matter how temporary it was. Even if Pearl agreed to it, I still didn't want it.

I'd rather die.

Cane knew that. I had no doubt he would make the right decision—even if that meant he would never see me again.

Chapter 3

PEARL

The world was spinning.

I couldn't stand on my own two feet.

No matter how many breaths I took, I wasn't getting enough air.

My heart was beating so fast I thought I'd have a heart attack.

So many tears.

The sobs. They made my chest hurt.

He told me he loved me before he disappeared. His tracker had shut off. I was completely in the dark in another country. My husband was captured, probably suffering every single moment as it passed.

I waited to wake up from this nightmare, but it never ended.

I called Cane over and over but could never get through

to him. I hoped that meant he was in the middle of getting Crow back. I hoped he was putting a bullet in between Tristan's eyes at that very moment. I hoped he was doing everything he possibly could to save my husband—the love of my life.

Lars sat beside me on the patio. The night had passed, and it was a beautiful and sunny day in Greece. But to me, I was in the middle of the biggest storm in history. The ship was sinking, and I didn't think we'd survive.

Lars wrapped his hand around mine and held it on the cushion, doing the only thing he could to comfort me. I'd hugged Lars once or twice over the years, but we'd never touched this way. And I knew why.

He was scared.

I cried on and off as the hours passed. Not knowing what was going on was the worst part. I wanted to take off to Italy, but I wasn't sure what help I would be. The reason Crow sent me away was to protect me. It would make all of his efforts pointless if I handed myself over to the people he was protecting me from.

My phone rang, and Cane's name popped up on the screen.

I answered instantly. "Please tell me you got him. Tell me he's okay. Please…"

Cane's silence was the most painful answer.

I started to cry.

"I'm working on it, Pearl," he said calmly. "Losing that

signal has made things more difficult. But I promise you, I won't stop until I find him."

"You have to get him back."

"I will, Pearl."

"I can't live without him…" I sobbed between my words, an emotional wreck. "I can't. You have to get him back."

"I know," he whispered. "I will. I know he's still in Italy. I've contacted all the air traffic controllers, and no private planes have taken off in the last day. So I think they're hiding nearby."

"You need to narrow it down more."

"I know."

"What does he want, Cane?" I whispered. "Does he want Adelina?" I didn't want to turn that woman over to the devil, not after everything we did to save her. But I didn't want to lose my husband either. We'd both suffered so much. We just wanted a quiet life in the countryside where we could raise our child. Apparently, that was too much to ask.

Cane was quiet for nearly a minute. "No, he doesn't want Adelina."

"Then what is it? Money?" I asked. "Crow put everything into an offshore account. I can get all of that for you, and you can hand it over to him."

"He doesn't want money."

"Then, what?" I pressed. "Whatever it is, just give it to him."

Cane sighed. "Pearl, he wants you."

The words fell on my shoulders like a ton of bricks. I felt the flood of fear, remembering the way Tristan looked at me when I went to his compound. He eye-fucked me then, and he wanted to make his fantasies a reality. He wanted to punish both Cane and Crow for crossing him. Taking me was the best way to accomplish that. Cane didn't need to spell it out for me.

In any other situation, I would have agreed to the trade in a heartbeat. I'd been a prisoner before, and I could do it again. I would find a way to escape, or Crow would find a way to rescue me. But now that I was pregnant, that wasn't an option. Crow couldn't protect our child.

I was the only one who could.

"I would...but I can't." My voice cracked. "Not with—"

"I know. Crow would never want that. I can't make the trade. I know my brother...and he'd rather die."

I knew that too. "You can't give up, Cane."

"Never. I'm supposed to give my answer to Tristan in eight hours. I'm afraid he'll kill Crow the second I say yes."

He might. "I would leave to help you, but I can't make it back in time."

"No," he said firmly. "Crow wants you there. You aren't leaving. I'm sure the only thing keeping him sane right now is knowing that you're safe. Trust me."

I knew that too. "Then what are we going to do? We

need to figure out where he is. How do you plan to narrow it down?"

Cane's silence was disturbing.

"You must have something."

"I think he's in Rome, but it's a pretty big place. It's hard to narrow it down."

"Ask people in contact with Tristan."

"I have," he said. "They haven't heard from him since his compound was destroyed. He purposely laid low so he could take us out like this. Tristan is pissed. That much is clear."

Which meant he was doing terrible things to Crow. "There has to be something…"

Cane was quiet, thinking furiously over the phone.

My mind was drawing a blank, but that was because I didn't do this sort of thing. Cane and Crow had been part of the underworld their entire lives. They knew how their enemies thought, knew their moves before they made them. I had nothing to offer other than the fact that I knew Crow the best.

What would he do?

"I guess I could do a satellite scan," Cane said. "But by the time we get all the images, we won't have much time to do anything with them."

An idea came to mind. "If they're in Rome, Crow probably knows exactly where they are."

"I guess," Cane said. "Assuming they didn't pull a sack over his head."

"Why would they cover his face if they're planning on killing him?" I hated to talk that way, but it had to be said.

"It's possible. But what's your point?"

"If you could talk to Crow, he could probably tell you where he is."

Cane sighed over the phone. "That would never happen. Tristan isn't going to let that happen."

"Just hear me out."

"I don't see the point."

"Shut up and listen. Tell Tristan that you agree to the trade, but you don't know where I am. Only Crow does."

"I know we're both stressed out right now, but that's stupid. Crow knows I would never make this trade—not in a million years. If the situation were reversed and I was the one in there, he would let me die instead of handing my wife over."

"Exactly."

"What?" he asked incredulously. "What point did you just make?"

"When he tells Crow that you agreed to the trade, Crow will know you're lying."

"Hmm…"

"Because he knows you would never do that to him. He knows you would never hand me over to Tristan."

"Even so, then what?"

"You tell Tristan that Crow will only give up the coordinates if you talk to him personally. You'll need to persuade him. Tristan will listen in on the conversation, obviously.

But Crow might be able to give you hints of where he's at without Tristan realizing it."

"What if Crow doesn't have any hints?"

"Then he just won't say anything. But if he does give you some bogus location, then we'll know he gets what we're trying to do."

Cane mulled over my words before he responded. "It's crazy…but it could work."

"We don't have any other options. I know Crow. He's been looking for an escape route ever since he got there. He would have taken in every single detail if he thought it could help him."

"You're right."

"So, we're going to do this?"

"Yeah," Cane said. "I think it's our best option. I'm gonna take the men to Rome because I think that's where Tristan is hiding. That way, we can move in quickly if Crow gives us any information."

"Okay." God, I hoped this worked. This was the only ploy we had up our sleeves. If it didn't work, I would lose Crow forever. I would raise our child alone, a widow who would be lost. It didn't matter that Crow prepared everything for me to be taken care of. All the money made no difference without him beside me. I would never get remarried because I believed in one love per lifetime—and he was mine.

"Pearl, I promise I'll do everything I can to get him back—even if that means taking a bullet for him."

I knew Cane loved Crow as much as I did, just in a different way.

"And if I can't, you know I'll be there for both of you until my last breath."

I knew that too. "Let's not talk that way. I can barely breathe as it is."

Chapter 4

CANE

I still hadn't spoken to Adelina since I left the house yesterday.

There hadn't been any time.

Now I was on my way to Rome, driving in one of the black Hummers that was completely bulletproof. I was alone for the drive with endless thoughts swirling in my brain. I had to get my brother out of there. Failure wasn't an option this time.

My phone rang through the car, and one of my other cell phone numbers popped up.

I knew who it was. "Hey." I hadn't had much time to think about the uncomfortable conversation we had the other day. I'd put my heart on the table, making it vulnerable by pulling it out of my body. I'd sacrificed everything for this woman. At that very moment, my brother was a prisoner because he risked his neck to save the woman I loved…while his own wife and child were in hiding. Now I felt like an idiot for putting him in danger.

"Hey, are you okay?" Adelina spoke with a beautiful voice, the kind that filled my dreams as I slept beside her. I loved the concern in her tone, the way she was affectionate with me while saying so little. I just wished it meant more.

"I'm in the middle of a nightmare. Crow has been captured. I'm on my way to Rome right now to break him out… I'm just not sure if I can pull this off."

"No…"

"Tristan took him."

"Pearl is still safe, right?"

"Yeah. She's not coming home yet."

"What are you going to do?" Adelina asked. "Is there anything I can do to help?"

"No." Just talking to her now was messing with my brain. A part of me resented her for not telling me she loved me. After everything I'd done for her, how could she not feel the same way? I wasn't Prince Charming, but I obviously cared for her. I knew I was a criminal and I took her as payment, but that didn't make me a bad guy. "I can't talk right now. I'll call when everything is over."

"Okay…please save him. He's a good man."

The best, actually. "I'll do everything I can. I can't let Pearl be a widow. Crow is more scared of that than actually dying."

"I know how much he loves her. I see it on his face every day."

And I thought I saw how much she loved me. "I've gotta go."

"Please be careful, Cane. I need you to come back too."

"I'll try." I wanted to tell her I loved her just in case I didn't return. I wanted her to know how much she'd changed my life for the better. She humanized me, made me realize I was capable of being more than just a monster. But none of those confessions emerged, either because I was too proud to say them or I was scared I would only be met with her silence. "Bye, Adelina."

"Cane…"

I listened to the silence over the line, hoping she would say something I wanted to hear.

"Please come back."

I felt stupid for hoping she'd say more. I shouldn't have expected anything else. "Okay." I hung up so I didn't have to say goodbye again.

―――――

TRISTAN ANSWERED with his usual arrogance. "I hope I'm not going to have to kill Crow today. Seems like a waste of potential."

The second our lines were connected, the threats came spilling out. It wasn't something I wanted to think about, the light gone from my brother's eyes as he lay like a corpse on the floor. "I've thought a lot about it. Crow is the only family I have left. After our war with Bones, I don't have anything left."

"Family is everything. I'm glad you see it that way."

"Crow won't want to trade his wife for his freedom."

"Yes, he mentioned that. Seemed pretty stubborn about it. But that's where you come in. Are you going to make this happen, Cane? Are you going to let your brother be tortured to death? I already started the process. Haven't heard him scream once."

The blood drained from my limbs. Torture, violence, and blood didn't faze me. But picturing my brother as the victim made me sway as I sat upright. "My brother would be angry if he knew I was doing this. But I have a problem."

"Make it go away," he said simply.

"You don't understand. I don't know where Pearl is." I did my best to sound convincing. I was lying through my teeth, but I'd never lied so convincingly before. There was a lot at stake here. If Tristan suspected this was all a ploy, he would kill Crow to spite me.

"You don't know?"

"He never told me. He didn't tell anyone."

"And you can't call her?"

"She won't tell me where she is. She destroyed her phone, so I can't trace her location."

Tristan fell silent.

He knew how close we were. He might not go for it.

"Then I'll have to kill him. That's too bad."

"If you let me talk to him, I can get him to tell me where she is."

"Doubtful. He's held up pretty well under torture."

I swallowed the bile back down my throat. "It's different with us. I can persuade him. If you've already exhausted him, he might be more likely to tell me. If you really want Pearl, this is the only way it's going to happen. I have to get my brother out of there, so I'm not gonna stop until I get that location."

Tristan considered what I said during a long pause. "And this isn't some tactic to speak to him?"

He wasn't as dumb as I hoped. "I'm sure you'll monitor the conversation, Tristan. I'd expect nothing less."

Tristan fell into a lengthy silence, his breathing hardly noticeable over the line. He was considering what I said, going over it from every possible angle. It wasn't impossible to believe Crow wouldn't tell me where Pearl was. Crow thought of every possibility, and he could have anticipated this situation. "Alright. I'll let you speak to him. But if I get the slightest suspicion you're up to something, I'll shoot him in the back of the head. You understand?"

I'd have to be even more careful. "Got it. Put him on the phone."

"WAKE HIM UP." Tristan's voice sounded in the background. "He's got a phone call."

I doubted he was asleep. He'd probably been knocked out sometime today. Hopefully, he would be coherent enough to understand what I was trying to do. Crow was much more intelligent than I was. If anyone could pick up on the plan, it was him.

"It's your brother," Tristan announced. "Do anything stupid, and you're dead." The phone became muffled, and sounds were heard as it was adjusted and placed on a flat surface. The speakerphone must have been initiated because it sounded different.

Here went nothing. "Crow, it's Cane."

"What?" Crow barked in annoyance, probably because Tristan told him what I wanted. Maybe he was angry because he actually thought I was trying to swap him for Pearl. Or maybe he was just in a lot of pain.

"Tristan told me the only way I can get you out of there is if Pearl takes your place." I did all the talking right in the beginning so Crow would pick up on what I was trying to do. "I didn't want to do it at first, but I realize you're the only other Barsetti I've got in the world. I've got to get you out of there—"

"Fuck you, Cane. I'd rather die a million times than let her take my place."

I pressed on so he wouldn't say anything else. "You need to tell me where she's at. You're the only person who knows where she is, and I know you won't tell Tristan. But you need to tell me. I know you love her, but she wouldn't want this. Pearl wouldn't want you to suffer. I don't want you to suffer. Just because Pearl would belong to Tristan doesn't mean she would die. It just means…"

"Don't say it," Crow said in a terrifying voice.

"It's not worth dying over, Crow." I hoped he understood the relevance of my statement. I knew exactly where she was. I knew what island she was on, and I knew the address to the place if I needed to go get her. There was no way I could have simply forgotten, not when he put it on a flash drive for me.

"No."

"Crow——"

"No."

Hopefully, he wasn't so delirious with pain that he couldn't think straight. Hopefully, they didn't hit his head too hard. Otherwise, he was extremely convincing.

"I can't live without you, man. You're my brother. I need you…"

Crow ignored my affectionate words. "Pearl is more important. If you really cared about my life that much, you wouldn't have asked me to free Adelina. If you really cared that much about protecting me, I wouldn't be here in the first place."

He would never say that to me under ordinary circumstances, even if he thought it. He'd definitely picked up on what I was doing. "I'm sorry. Now I'm doing what I can to get you out."

"Pearl has already suffered. When she was a prisoner to Bones, he did terrible things to her. The bruises, the broken bones, the trauma…it's a miracle she didn't lose her mind. I'm not letting another man repeat those actions."

Crow hated talking about Bones. He never even said his name. To go into detail about her captivity didn't make any sense. He was definitely trying to tell me something. But what was it?

"I'm not letting that happen again," he repeated. "So this is it. This is the last time we'll ever speak."

"Crow, come on. Just tell me."

"Forget it."

Tristan and the other men in the room didn't interrupt. Tristan was probably hoping Crow would give in and hand over the address. Having Pearl would be the greatest revenge Tristan could possibly have. It would hurt both Crow and me.

"Remember when we were kids, and Dad took us to that coffee shop down the street from the Colosseum?"

We'd never done anything like that in our lives. "Yeah. You stole that pack of gum from underneath the register, and Dad spanked your ass for it. But he also spanked mine for tattling on you." I had to make it more convincing that we weren't speaking in a coded message. I knew Crow was trying to tell me exactly where he was.

Crow released a faint chuckle. "Yeah. He knew what he was doing. And he taught me what it means to be a brother… I'll never forget that."

"Crow, you know what's going to happen if you don't tell me where she is. I'm telling you, Pearl would want this."

Crow was silent.

"She would rather suffer for the rest of her life than let you die."

Again, silence.

"Goddammit, Crow. Just tell me. Would you really deny your wife's wishes?" I had to make this convincing, and Crow couldn't give in too easily. If he did, it would be obvious this was just a ploy.

"I'm supposed to protect her. If I give her up, I'd be worthless."

"Not if she wants you to. Marriage is a two-way street. This way, you both get to live."

Crow was quiet.

"Please."

Nothing.

"I need you, Crow. Don't make me be the only Barsetti left."

"You can carry on our legacy, Cane."

"No, I can't," I snapped. "I'm not the better brother. You are. I should be in that chair right now. I should be the one being held as a prisoner. I can't live with this guilt, Crow. I can't live knowing I'm the reason you…" I didn't finish the sentence.

Crow didn't say anything else.

There was silence, which was followed by more silence.

I continued to wait for him to make a move.

But nothing came.

"We're running out of time, Crow. Just tell——"

"Serengeti, Tanzania."

It was a random place, and the exact opposite direction of Pearl. It was remote and unremarkable, which made it believable.

"She's staying at the Four Seasons," Crow whispered.

I knew he was in Rome, somewhere close to the Colosseum. He also mentioned Bones, who had lived in Rome. Those were the two clues, and once I looked at a map, I'd probably be able to narrow it down.

The plan worked.

Tristan took the phone. "I'll send men to fetch her now. But I'm not letting him go until she's in my custody." He hung up without giving me the opportunity to say another word.

I grabbed my laptop and did some research into the area. I identified the coffee shop Crow had mentioned, and I also put in the coordinates of Bones's residence. It was fifteen miles to the east, so that didn't narrow it down enough.

Then I realized he was talking about a different address.

Bones's factory.

I entered that in next. Between the coffee shop and his warehouse, there was just a single road. The road led to an abandoned compound with old warehouses. The property had been purchased by a hotel company, and it was going to be built for tourists.

Now I knew where he was.

It was time to get my brother out of there.

———

WE MET at a rendezvous point two miles away so we wouldn't arouse the suspicion of Tristan and his men. Crow was smart to pick a location that was at least a twenty-hour plane ride away. They wouldn't figure out Crow was lying for at least ten hours, at the earliest.

Bran was in one of the Hummers parked in the alleyway, speaking to the tech guys back on the base. He was waiting for a scan of the area to determine the lay of the land. I assumed Tristan only had a few men working for him, but I'd rather be safe than sorry.

I had shit to do, but I knew it was my obligation to call Pearl. She was undoubtedly a mess right now, alternating between pacing and sobbing. The phone barely rang once before she answered. "What happened?"

"Your idea worked."

"It did?" she blurted into the phone, slightly maniacal. "What does that mean? Did you find his location?"

"Crow dropped hints and helped me pinpoint his location."

"Where is he?" she demanded.

"Rome."

"Then why are you on the phone with me? Go get him, Cane." She was more ruthless and aggressive than I'd ever heard her. Even when I first met her, she wasn't nearly as fiery. All of her emotions were heightened when it came to Crow.

"We're doing a satellite sweep of the area. We need to know what we're up against. We have time. Crow told them you were in Africa, so it'll take a while before they figure out he's full of shit."

"We have time?" she hissed. "Crow is in there suffering, and you think we have time?"

The only reason I was putting up with her shit was because this was my fault in the first place. "We have to do this right, Pearl—for his sake. I'm certain we didn't tip off Tristan, so we're going to hit him hard."

"Don't kill him."

I cocked my head even though we weren't talking face-to-face. "What?"

"I want to kill that asshole myself. I want to look him in the eye and shoot him right in the skull. He took my husband from me, and no one fucks with a Barsetti like that." She even had a slight Italian accent as she said it. "He tried to hurt my family. He threatened to hurt me. I want to kill him, Cane."

I knew she was just angry right now, not that I judged her for it. She had it in her. She'd stabbed Bones without thinking twice about it. She wanted revenge for what Tristan had done to Crow. I didn't tell her Crow had already been tortured because that would just hurt her. But I knew letting her kill Tristan wasn't a good idea. "I can't do that, Pearl. I have to kill everyone in that complex. No one gets out alive."

"Then you'd better let Crow do it," she hissed. "That man tried to come between us. He deserves to pull the trigger."

I deserved to pull the trigger as much as either of them after what Tristan did to Adelina, but that wasn't appropriate to say right now. "I'll see what happens when I'm in there."

"Do not let him get away, Cane. I mean it."

"I know, Pearl."

She sighed into the phone, announcing all of her stress in the single sound. "I'm sorry… I'm just so scared. I can't stop thinking about what they're doing to him. I keep crying. I can't stop." A few quiet sobs erupted over the line.

The same fears plagued me too. "I can promise you there's nothing they could do to Crow to hurt him. That guy is made of steel. He's the strongest guy I've ever known. They may not have even done anything to him. Tristan thinks he got what he wanted, so there's no reason to antagonize Crow." It was effortless for me to lie because I was doing it for the right reason. Crow would want me to keep her calm, especially since she was carrying his kid. "I'll let you know when we're about to move in."

"Okay," she whispered. "Please don't take too long. I might have a heart attack. I'm usually so calm about things but…I just can't relax. I'm losing my mind."

"It's okay," I said. "I know how you feel about him.

You've never been scared when your own life is at risk because you're brave. But when it comes to someone else, it's much more terrifying."

"God, now I know how he feels when I do stupid shit."

I normally would chuckle, but I wasn't in the mood. "Yeah."

She sniffled over the line. "Tell me when it's done. Put him on the phone…I need to hear his voice."

"I promise."

"Okay…" She hung up.

I stuffed my phone back into my pocket and walked to the Hummer where Bran was. He was in the back with the tech gear and staring at the computer screen. "You got anything?"

"Yeah…but it's not good."

"Why do you say that?" He had more men than we realized? He wasn't in the location that Crow gave us?

Bran pulled up the satellite feed of the area, picking up heat-generated sensors that showed the dynamics of the compound. All the warehouses had people inside, silhouettes of people working. "I think all of these men are Tristan's….and there are nearly a hundred of them."

"They could just be neighbors."

"Unlikely." Bran zoomed in on one of the images, the stacks of cargo and the way the facility was outlined. "I think this is where he keeps the shipments of weapons he bought from you."

"Why would he have us deliver them to France if he brought them back to Italy?"

"No idea. But I don't know what else he would be keeping. I doubt two different clans of criminals are working in such close proximity to each other. Also…" He pulled up another image. "I dug this up from government records. The compound is being bought by a hotel company."

"I saw the same thing."

"But if you look at the deed of trust…it has Tristan's name on it."

My heart fell into my stomach. "Shit."

"So, he owns all of this. I doubt he's renting it out to someone."

"Fuck."

"So we're up against at least a hundred men…all of whom are heavily armed."

I had to sit down because the news was depressing. It was a blow to the head, chest, and heart. My brother wasn't surrounded by a few dozen men. Tristan outnumbered us ten to one.

I didn't like those odds.

"You know I'd do anything for Crow, but this is a suicide mission."

I couldn't deny that.

"Our only option is to bomb the entire place, but that would be counterproductive since Crow wouldn't survive either."

I stared at the screen and tried to search for an answer

to my problem. Doing nothing wasn't an option. Even if I died, I had to try to get Crow out of there. I would never forgive myself for turning the other cheek. And Pearl wouldn't forgive me either.

"I don't see a way around this," Bran said. "It will take weeks to find enough men to pull this off."

"I know…"

"I can probably pinpoint Crow's location and we could attempt to sneak in, but it looks like he has guards posted all over the place."

"Yeah."

"You got any ideas?"

I dragged my hands down my face and cupped my mouth. "No."

"Well, you better think of something quick. We only have a few hours until they figure out Crow is lying. And Tristan will definitely kill him, then."

I covered my face and tried not to give in to the panic. "I know."

———

I MADE a few phone calls and tried to round up as many men as I could, but I only managed to pick up a few dozen. I was still down by half, and that wasn't enough to storm the compound. These men would lay down their lives if they thought they had good odds, but in this case, it was still a mission doomed to fail.

I might have to go in there alone.

I was at a stalemate and didn't know what to do. The person I would normally turn to was Crow, but he wasn't there. I called Crewe Donoghue, a friend of ours in Scotland, but he didn't have enough time to send me the aid I needed.

I was screwed.

I was running out of time but had no idea what to do next. I called Adelina, needing someone to talk to. She wasn't my first pick, but at least she was someone. Pearl wasn't an option. If I told her about our problem, she would have a meltdown.

"Is everything over?" Adelina asked the second our lines were connected. "Is he okay?"

"I haven't moved in yet. I know where he's at, but Tristan's got at least a hundred men in the compound and unlimited ammunition. I don't know what to do. I've commissioned as many men as possible, but it's still not enough..." I leaned against the wall of the alleyway and stared at the puddle of water sitting at my feet. "I'll go in alone if I have to, but that's not going to end well. We'll both be dead."

"Please don't say that," she whispered.

I didn't care about sparing her feelings. This was reality. This was the truth. I'd thought getting Crow out of there would be simple. I thought we'd already be done by now. But now that seemed impossible. "I've never been so scared..."

"What does Pearl think?"

"I can't call her."

"Why not?" she asked. "She has no idea what's going on?"

"No. She's the one who told me to pretend to hand her over. It was a good idea. But now she thinks I'm moving in to get him at this very moment. I can't call her and tell her there's no hope. I can't listen to that woman cry…especially since she never cries."

"Cane, this is too important to keep her in the dark. You can't spare her feelings. If Crow dies, she's going to feel all that pain anyway."

"I'd rather protect her for as long as possible…"

"She gave you that idea. Maybe she can help you find a solution."

"Pearl is smart, but she's not a criminal mastermind."

"You need to give her more credit. I know exactly what she went through, and neither one of us is weaker because of it. We are stronger, more powerful. We both have experience you lack. She might have something to offer."

Adelina was right. "Maybe…"

"I wasn't with Tristan very long, but I know he's not stupid. He's very paranoid, and I've heard him speak on the phone to his associates. He plans things far in advance, and he's a lot smarter than he seems. I wouldn't be surprised if he wanted you to break Crow out."

"He has no idea I know where he is."

"Or does he?" she challenged. "The only reason you

wiped out his compound is because he thought you weren't going to hand me over in the first place. He had all of his men armed and ready to attack in France before you pulled up to the compound. He told me himself. He expected you to keep me. The only reason you got me out of there was because he never anticipated you would do it."

He was smarter than I gave him credit for.

"I wouldn't be surprised if he anticipated all of this, and he's waiting for you to move in, assuming he only has a few men by his side. He probably wants to wipe out both of you for good. As long as one of you is still alive, he'll always have to look over his shoulder. Speaking in code to Crow sounds too easy, if you ask me."

Now my heart was pounding. Adelina was making sense —completely.

"That's my input. Now you should ask Pearl for hers. She knows how psychopaths work. She was a prisoner a lot longer than I was."

I didn't want to bring Pearl this terrible news, but I knew it was unavoidable. I needed every bit of insight if I were going to pull this off. Adelina just gave me a perspective that I hadn't anticipated. I was too stressed out to critically evaluate the situation—that I was being played. "I'll call her."

"I think that's a good idea. I hope it works out."

"Me too." I hung up and called Pearl.

She answered before the phone even rang. "Is he okay? Did you get him?"

I hated to disappoint her. "I haven't moved in yet."

"Oh…" Her depression was heavy in the words.

"I've run into some complications."

"No, please don't say that to me." Her voice started to crack again.

"I spoke to Adelina, and she thinks Tristan might be setting me up. He knows my conversation with Crow meant more than we let on, and he's waiting for me to show up. Bran looked at the satellite footage, and Tristan has a hundred armed men in the compound."

"No man has an army unless he's expecting a war. I think Adelina is right." Her voice was full of sorrow, but she didn't burst into tears like last time.

"I'm starting to think she is too. He probably thinks I'll break in to the compound with twelve men. Then he'll slaughter us."

"You need more men, Cane."

"I've called everyone I know. I only managed to pick up twenty more men."

"That's not enough."

"I know. I'll go in there alone if I have to…but I know it'll kill me."

"There's a solution to every problem. Crow always tells me that."

"I wish he were here… He would know what to do."

She sighed into the phone. "But we're all he has, Cane. And we're getting him out of there one way or another. We aren't giving up."

"Never."

"Then you need to think of something, Cane. And think fast." Her usual strength resurfaced, the attitude Crow noticed when he first saw her. She turned hard and fierce, knowing she didn't have time to shed a single tear when Crow's life was on the line.

"I've thought of everything, Pearl."

"If you had, we would have a plan right now."

"I've called everyone I know. Even if I could make it back to our base in Florence, I wouldn't have enough men to bring all our weapons and trucks. The issue is the number of men. I just don't have enough."

"Then you need to find them."

"I already told you I called everyone. I even called some of Crow's contacts too."

"There's gotta be somebody…"

I wished there were.

"What about money? What if we offer him everything we have?"

"He doesn't care about money, Pearl. This is personal now. I could offer him a hundred million, and he wouldn't blink an eye."

"Then we have nothing else to offer…except me."

"We aren't even going to talk about that."

When Pearl didn't argue, I knew she agreed with me. The second Tristan realized she was pregnant, he would kill the baby. Pearl couldn't let that happen. I couldn't let that happen to my future niece or nephew.

We had to protect that child no matter what. "Wait…"

"What?" Maybe Adelina was right, and Pearl would have a trick up her sleeve.

"Crow mentioned your beef with the Skull Kings. They're trying to push you out of the market."

How was that relevant? "Not important right now, Pearl."

"It is important. Aren't they the biggest assassins in the world?"

They were ruthless, merciless, and terrifying. "I wouldn't fuck with them, if that's what you're asking."

"They want the business. It sounds like they aren't going to stop until they get it."

"Again, I don't see the point of this."

"They are exactly what we need right now, Cane. They have the means to get this done. They probably have all the men, and they obviously have the weapons. They could be the leverage we need."

"They wouldn't help me, Pearl. They aren't the kind of crew that does favors."

"You wouldn't ask them for a favor, Cane. You would make an exchange with them. Crow's life for the business."

I felt the bomb explode inside my chest once she made the suggestion. It was a great idea, but something I didn't want to do. Crow and I had argued about this a few times. He wanted to give up the business and live a quiet life. It wasn't worth the war the Skull Kings would bring on us.

But it was all I had, my life's work. My father ran the business his whole life until we inherited it. The woman I loved didn't love me back, so I had nothing else to commit my life to. The business wasn't just about money. It was about identity.

"Cane?"

I heard her voice even though my mind was spinning at a million miles an hour.

"What are you thinking?"

"Um…" I didn't know what I was thinking. I felt like an ass for hesitating at all.

"Are you going to contact them?"

There should be no doubt in my mind. Our father's legacy didn't matter anymore. All we had was each other. That was the important thing. I could live without my work, but I couldn't live without my brother. "I'll call them now."

Chapter 5

CROW

Any minute now, I would be rescued.

Cane would storm the compound with our men, kill Tristan, and release the ropes that bound my wrists together. I would see my wife again, meet my son or daughter. I would hold Button until she finally stopped crying. When I retrieved her from Greece, I might stay for a few weeks—take an extended vacation.

I just had to hold on a little longer.

Dried blood was caked down my face, my head was still pounding, my gut screamed from the internal injuries I suffered.

But I was high—knowing this would end soon.

Cane was a genius when he called me. He figured out a way to get the information he needed without having my tracker. He didn't give up on me. At any moment, he would risk his life to get me out of there.

The door opened, and Tristan walked inside, his sneer now raised into a smile. One of his men set the chair in front of me so he could take a seat. "You want to know what your brother's biggest flaw is?"

I stared at him, only one eye functioning.

"Arrogance. He thinks no one can outsmart him. And you know what? You're arrogant too."

I stayed silent, knowing a conversation was pointless. Sometime in the next few hours, Tristan would be dead. I'd be the one looking down at his corpse—and spitting on it.

"You think I don't know what that conversation was really about."

The high I felt suddenly evaporated like a drop of water in a hot pan. I did my best to control my reaction, and the only reason I was successful was from years of practice. I had the best poker face in the business, but my skills were seriously being tested in that moment.

"You think I underestimated the Barsetti bond?" he asked. "I knew Cane was full of shit. I knew he was just trying to figure out where you were. I'm glad. Because he's going to roll in here with a few men—while I have a hundred. I'm gonna blow that asshole to hell. Once I'm done with him, I'll kill you. Adelina will be easy to track down, and eventually, I'll find that gorgeous wife of yours."

Adrenaline spiked in my blood, and I wondered if I had

enough rage to break through the ropes and chains that bound me. I wanted to rip his chair in half then beat him to death with it. But there was still a possibility that he thought Cane was telling the truth, so I didn't change my reaction. I swallowed my anger and hoped I'd get my revenge somehow. Cane was smart. I just hoped he was smart enough to realize he was walking into a trap. He had to stay alive. He had to protect Adelina as well as my wife—and my future child.

Now I was scared of losing Pearl all over again.

She was safe in Greece, protected by my best men. She had the paperwork to keep her in hiding as long as she wanted. But if Tristan didn't give up, he might find her one day. She might be stupid and take a trip to the mall alone. Tristan might look at her kid and realize how similar it looked to me. Thankfully, no one knew she was pregnant besides Cane, Lars, and me.

Tristan continued to examine me, waiting for me to take a bite of the bait he placed on the hook. "Your face hasn't changed, but I know your heart is racing. Your eyes are the same, but there's fear in there—deep down inside. That's exactly what I wanted."

"Did you send men to Serengeti?"

His eyes narrowed.

"Now look who's arrogant. I told you the truth, and you didn't believe me. Cane isn't coming, and my wife is vulnerable. Now all you're doing is wasting time."

Tristan continued to give me that aggressive look with a crooked sneer. He rose from the chair and kicked it over. "I can't wait to fuck your wife in her mouth, her pussy, and her ass."

Chapter 6

CANE

Constantine answered the phone with his usual act of strange indifference. "My favorite Barsetti. How's it going?" He'd never met my brother, so it didn't make sense for him to have a favorite. But Constantine was a bit of a nutjob in that way. He was always hanging off the edge, ready to turn in either direction. He was full of craziness, but he was also full of ruthless intelligence. It was the reason everyone hired him to do their dirty work. He had a mental hinge that allowed him to live a life free of remorse and guilt. I'd seen him gut a man like a fish then immediately eat lunch afterward, while the corpse was still warm and bleeding on the floor. "I've been better."

"That's too bad. Hope you aren't expecting me to fix your boo-boos."

"No. Actually, I have something for you."

"Indeed?" he asked, a smile in his voice. "You know there's only thing I want. I just haven't decided if I'm going to take it from you."

I'd been a brother to this man in my past. The fact that he considered me to be nothing more than a stranger hurt my pride. But I knew it was just the way he was programmed. He didn't feel camaraderie like the rest of us. He was built on a different foundation. "You can't take anything from me, Constantine. But I'm prepared to give it to you in exchange for something."

"A barter, huh? What do you have in mind?"

"I know you won't be able to turn it down."

"Then it must involve a lot of bloodshed."

"Actually, yes."

He grew quiet. "I'm listening."

"I have a job for you. I have an enemy I need to eliminate. You take him out for me, and my entire business is yours."

He was quiet again, his twisted thoughts working quickly. "All for one man? I hope you have a legitimate reason why you can't do this on your own."

"I do. This man is in a complex with a hundred soldiers. All heavily armed."

"Now we're talking…"

"He has my brother held captive. I need your crew to help mine take everyone out in the compound while I get my brother out of there. That's the job. It's big. There'll be a lot of casualties. But the trade is fair. Do we have a deal?"

Constantine took his time thinking to himself. He didn't say anything for nearly a minute. I was in a time crunch, but Constantine operated by his own rules. He couldn't be rushed or persuaded. "You need to be more specific."

"About what?"

"Who's the main target?"

"Tristan Clavern."

"Ah, yes. I know him. Never liked him."

"That makes two of us."

"So your entire business is mine, huh? Does that include everything?"

"It includes everything inside the warehouses, the supplies, the clients, everything. Your men can resume my business, and my clients don't even need to be aware of the change in ownership. But I suggest you don't fuck them over because they'll come after you."

"I'm a very honorable man…when it comes to business."

"Does that mean we have a deal?"

Constantine paused again, and this time, it seemed like he was drawing it out on purpose. "I think so. When is this going down?"

"In an hour."

"In an hour?" he asked incredulously.

"I know that's extremely short notice but—"

"I like it. The business has been getting too easy lately. Send me the location, and I'll meet you in thirty minutes."

Chapter 7

CROW

I was scared.

I couldn't lie to myself.

My brother's life was on the line. Button would never be safe if we both died. Adelina would be a prisoner again. My body would be thrown into the middle of the ocean so my remains would never be found.

My life had completely turned upside down since Cane asked me to save Adelina.

What if I had just said no?

What if I were in Greece with Button right now?

Would things have been better? Or would they be worse?

Could anything be worse than this?

Two guards stood on either side of the door at the entrance to the warehouse. The place was cold because the ventilation system must have stopped working ten years ago. The concrete was cracked in places as time and the earth made its mark. All I could do was sit there and keep waiting. The pain was agonizing, but it didn't seem important compared to the fear deep inside my chest.

Then I heard an explosion.

Cane was here.

Tristan's prediction was right on the nose. He knew Cane would come, but he was outnumbered. Even with all the resources we had, Cane didn't have enough men to wield the right firepower.

Hopefully, Cane would flee and get out of there alive. I needed him to take care of Button and the little Barsetti since I wouldn't be around to look after them. It wouldn't take long for my brother to figure out there was no possibility he could win this war.

The gunshots started. Yells erupted. Commands were issued. The two men on either side of the door ran out to join the fight since I wasn't going anywhere. It seemed like I was sitting in the middle of a war zone. Listening to the slaughter go on outside was worse than seeing it.

My imagination made it much worse.

Time seemed to slow down as I continued to listen to the bloodshed. I was surprised the battle wasn't over yet. It should have ended within two minutes. Cane and our men didn't stand a chance against everything Tristan had.

It was hopeless.

The door flew open, and Cane and Bran sprinted into the room.

What the hell?

"Watch the door." Cane darted to me, gave me a quick glance over as he checked my injuries, and then pulled out a knife.

"Tristan is ambushing you," I blurted. "He's got a hundred men posted around the compound."

"Don't worry about it." Cane cut the rope that bound my wrists together then moved to the chains around my ankles.

Bran remained at the door, covered in a bulletproof vest and a helmet. He wielded a large machine gun, ready to take down anyone who approached the entryway.

Cane couldn't pick the lock, so he pulled out his pistol and shot the chain right next to my foot. It snapped in half like a piece of pasta. "Can you walk?"

"Yeah. What about Tristan?"

"The men will take care of him. I have to get you out of here."

I yanked the rope off my hands and rose to my feet. I didn't even make it to my full height before I stumbled, my body staggering to the right. I didn't realize how weak I was, how much blood I lost, and what the dehydration had done to me.

"I got you." Cane pushed his shoulder underneath mine and held me up with his arm. "The chopper is going to land in five. They'll get you out of here." He supported me as we headed to the back door that was bolted shut.

"No." I stopped moving, gritting my teeth as I felt pain shooting up my leg. Tristan kicked me there this morning, and something had ripped. Every time I breathed, my broken ribs screamed in pain too. "I'm not leaving until I kill that fucker."

"Trust me, he won't make it out of this alive. We need to worry about you right now."

I moved away from his hold, but I could barely stand on my own two feet. I felt dizzy, light-headed, and overwhelmingly weak. "That asshole threatened to rape my wife. I'm not leaving until I have at least ten bullets in his brain." I felt my leg shake as I worked to support myself.

Cane wrapped my arm around his shoulder. "What's more important, Crow? Getting back to your wife and kid or getting your revenge?"

My rage needed to be satisfied, but I knew Button was terrified right now. She wanted to hear my voice. She didn't care how Tristan died. She just wanted me to be safe. I clenched my jaw as another jolt of pain ran up my body.

"I promise I'll get him, Crow." Cane escorted me to the door again, Bran still posted by the doorway.

"He knew," I said as I felt my ribs scream.

"Yeah, I know. Adelina told me he would have figured out our plan."

"Smart girl. Where did you get the men?"

"That's a long story." Cane got to the doorway and shot

off the hinges so he could kick the door down. "I'll tell you when we get into the chopper." The door flew open with a heavy thud, and the sound of gunshots became louder. We were blocked by another warehouse, and men were positioned in the center of the opening, ducking behind cars and buildings.

Cane swept the area before he crossed and took me behind the power plant, which looked like it'd been abandoned for ten years. I leaned against the wall and breathed through the pain.

Cane kept his eyes trained on our surroundings, his gun ready to fire. He tapped his ear. "Send in the chopper. Come from the west. Drop a ladder and don't land." Cane remained sharply focused, no longer looking at me because he kept checking our surroundings.

I saw the chopper in the distance, bulletproof and jet black.

"You're going to have to hold on to the ladder so they can get you out of here quicker. Once the men realize it's here, they'll probably try to shoot it down."

"What about you?"

"I'll stay behind and cover you."

"No."

Cane didn't look at me.

"We both get out."

"I'm not abandoning my men, Crow." He glanced at me before he turned away. "I have to make sure I kill Tristan, not just for you, but for Adelina. I know you would stay and help, but you're too injured. I got you into this mess, and I have to get you out."

"The chopper can carry us both."

"I'm not leaving," he said firmly. "I'll get out of this alive. Don't worry about me."

The chopper zoomed in at a high speed and dropped the rope ladder toward the ground. The rotors were loud, announcing the helicopter's presence to everyone within a mile radius.

"We don't have time, Crow. Go." Cane left my side and darted back into the mayhem. He ran along the wall, staying under cover as he rejoined the fight on the other side of the warehouse.

If I could physically do something, I'd grab a gun and join him. But I was too weak to do any damage. I would just get killed instead. Since I had a family waiting for me, that wasn't an option. I used the last of my energy to run and jump onto the rope ladder. I swung forward, toward the sky and underneath the helicopter.

They immediately flew off, carrying me away from the gunshots that could still be heard as we rose in height. My ribs screamed in pain, and the weakness from my limbs made it difficult to hold on, but I wrapped my arm around the rope and locked it into place. If I let go, I would dangle.

They started to reel me in, pulling me into the chopper as we flew over Rome and retreated to a safe location. When I reached the skids of the chopper, one of the men pulled me inside and shut the door. It was even louder in there, directly underneath the rotors.

"We're taking you to the hospital." He handed me a helmet with a radio so I could understand what he was saying.

I pulled myself into the seat and strapped myself into place, feeling my mind go fuzzy. "I need to talk to Pearl."

"Cane's orders are to get you medical attention. You can call her later."

She had to know I was okay. "Just give me your phone."

"We can't use it in here. You know that."

I ground my teeth and looked out the window, feeling the last of my energy slip away.

Chapter 8

Cane

The battle was over.

The bodies were piled behind the warehouse where they would be burned. The already run-down compound looked even worse now that we were finished with it. People in the area probably called the police when they heard the gunshots, but the police knew to look the other way. They knew we wouldn't cross them if they let us be. The citizens thought the police ran this country, but it was actually the criminals that controlled it.

"Found your little friend." Constantine emerged from the circle while dragging Tristan by the ankle. He pulled him along the pavement, a trail of blood smearing behind him. Tristan was still alive but seriously injured. Constantine dropped him right in front of me, wearing the same grin a demon would wear. "We're settled, then?"

"Yep."

"Tomorrow, we'll be at your base first thing in the morning. I expect everything to be in order."

"It will be."

He nodded to his comrades before he winked at me. "Have fun. Revenge has always gotten me off far better than a woman ever could." He walked away with his crew, heading to the vehicles scattered around the area. Some vehicles were on fire from the gunshots, and others were simply totaled.

I lost a few men, but most of us made it out of there alive.

Tristan wouldn't be able to say the same.

Tristan pulled himself up with weak arms. Blood dripped down his forehead and across his lips. His hair was matted with the wet blood that soaked into the strands. He sat up, slightly swaying with weakness.

I didn't feel an ounce of pity.

"What are you waiting for?" he said under his breath.

"I'm not waiting for anything." I pulled the pistol from the back of my jeans and cocked it. "Just enjoying it."

He narrowed his eyes in anger, but he still wouldn't show his terror.

"Now you know how it feels to be powerless, to have someone control you without your permission. Pretty shitty, huh?"

Tristan looked at one of the warehouses in the distance. "Isn't it strange to think we did business together for so long, and it was a single woman who changed all of that?"

She wasn't just a woman. She was my woman.

He shook his head. "I became obsessed with her the second I laid eyes on her. But I suspect your feelings are stronger than obsession. The only reason a man would go to such great lengths was if he loved her." He turned his gaze back to me. "So, I have to ask. Was she worth it?"

I raised the gun and aimed right between his eyes. I'd risked everything for this woman, but she didn't feel the same way. It hurt more than when my brother shot me. It hurt more than all the guilt I felt over beating Pearl. I'd never felt anything more than lust for a woman, and now I found a woman I would die for—but she wouldn't die for me. "Any last words?"

"You never answered my question." He stared down the barrel, unafraid despite what was about to happen. He would never see blue sky again. He would never feel the sunlight on his face.

My finger moved to the trigger. "Yes. And I would do it all over again."

Click.

———

I CALLED OLIVER, one of the guys who picked up Crow and took him to the hospital. "How is he?"

"We got him into the emergency room, and they immediately took him to surgery. Looks like he has some internal bleeding, along with broken ribs. He needed a blood transfusion because he lost so much."

"But he's going to be okay, right?"

"They didn't say," Oliver said. "But we're still here, so we can receive updates. What's going on over there?"

"Cleaning up and preparing to leave. Once this gets taken care of, I'll be there."

"Alright. He wanted to call Pearl, but by the time he got here, he'd passed out."

"I'll take care of it."

"Okay. Seemed important to him."

I hung up then prepared to call her. I thought I should call Adelina first because she was worried about me. I would feel so much satisfaction telling her that Tristan was dead. She would feel nothing but relief, knowing that her life was her own again. But Pearl was a mess, so Adelina could wait.

I called her.

Pearl picked up instantly, as if she was sitting by the phone just waiting for it to ring. "Please tell me he's okay." Emotion was in her voice again, terrified because I was the one calling her instead of Crow.

"He's okay."

"Oh…thank god." She exhaled over the line, her breath loud.

"Tristan is dead. All of his men are gone. Crow is at the hospital right now. He's in surgery."

"No…"

"He had some——"

"I don't want to know."

I turned silent, knowing his afflictions would break her heart.

"Just tell me he's going to be okay."

"I don't know for sure, but I feel certain he'll be fine. He wasn't shot or anything."

"I'm coming back. I need to be at that hospital."

"I…I'm not sure if he would want you to leave, Pearl."

"You said Tristan is dead, along with all of his men, right?"

"Yeah."

"Then I'm not sitting on my ass any longer. My husband needs me, so I'm leaving."

"His men won't allow you to leave until he gives them the order."

"Then you override it, Cane," she snapped. "Because one way or another, I'm getting out of here."

"Okay, fine," I said. "I'm sure he'd want to see you anyway."

"I'm gonna pack my stuff, then. They better be ready by the time I'm done."

"Okay."

"And thank you, Cane. Thank you for saving my husband."

Her gratitude only made me feel terrible. "Please don't thank me. This is all my fault…"

"But now all of us are free. You did that, Cane."

"I shouldn't have risked my brother's life like that, not for a woman."

"She's not just some woman, Cane. You love her."

I closed my eyes at the comment. "But she doesn't love me…"

Pearl was quiet, obviously unsure what to say.

"I wanted to save her regardless, but I wouldn't have gotten my brother involved if that was how she felt. I feel stupid. I risked everything for that woman."

Pearl was still quiet. It would be impossible to come up with a good response to that. The only reason why I told her was because the aftershocks of the situation were hitting me hard. My brother was in the hospital, my sister was in Greece, Adelina was at home wondering what happened to me.

"I'm not sure I believe that."

"Believe what?" I whispered.

"That she doesn't love you. I spent time with her, and every time she talked about you, her eyes lit up. She had nothing but good things to say, even when she could have been completely honest with me. Give her some time. I think she'll come around."

"I think you're wrong, Pearl. But thanks for trying to make me feel better."

Her sigh filled the phone. "Tristan is dead, huh?"

"Yeah."

"Are you sure?"

"Shot him between the eyes myself."

"Good," she said with anger. "You gave him an execution he didn't deserve. Should have tortured him the way he tortured Crow."

"I just wanted to end it. The world is already a little more beautiful without him in it."

"Yeah...I guess."

"I should get going, Pearl. I need to call Adelina."

"Okay. Make sure you talk to Crow's men about getting me out of here."

"I will."

She hung up.

I called Adelina next, feeling my heart pound as the phone rang. She must have found one of my other phones in the house, and I hoped she still had it on her so I could reach her.

She answered a few rings later. "I'm so glad you're okay."

When I listened to that concern in her voice, it made me soften. There was nothing better than having a woman like her care about me, one who wanted to hear my voice as much as I wanted to hear hers. Women used to mean only one thing to me—sex. But Adelina represented that and so much more. "Tristan is dead."

"He is?" she asked with a gasp. "You're sure?"

"I shot him myself."

"Wow..." She took a moment to process what I said, to accept the fact that her tormentor was really gone.

"I killed the rest of his men too. No one will ever come after you again."

"I...I don't know what to say. I don't even know how to process this. I haven't been free in so long that I'm not even sure what it feels like anymore."

"You're free now, *Bellissima.*"

She breathed into the phone, the emotion obvious but the tears absent. "How's Crow? Tell me he's alright."

"He's in surgery right now. Had some internal bleeding."

"No...poor Pearl."

"She's flying back today so she can see him."

"You think he'll be okay?"

I really had no idea. "He's the strongest man I've ever known. If anyone will get through it, it's him."

"Yeah."

"I'm gonna head over there once I'm finished here. That surgery is going to be at least a few hours. I should be there before he wakes up."

"Can I come along?"

I'd love to see her and wrap my arms around her. I'd love to kiss her and to enjoy the peace that we both had now. "I would go get you, but it's a long drive. I should get to the hospital as soon as I can."

"I understand," she whispered. "I can't wait to see you."

"I can't wait to see you either." When she wormed her way into my heart so easily, it didn't surprise me that I fell for her. She hypnotized me with her affection, made me weak and want to crumble.

"You aren't hurt, right?"

"Just a few scratches."

"Good."

"I should get going. I'll give you an update when I can."

"Okay…but I have a question."

"Okay."

"I think I already know the answer to this since you haven't mentioned it, but…do you know what happened to Lizzie?"

I didn't have the heart to say the words out loud. I didn't want to hurt Adelina with the truth. Her friend had suffered a much worse fate than she did. She was beaten every single day until they took it too far and killed her. I would never tell her that Crow found her body wrapped in a plastic bag in preparation to release into the sea. I would never share the description he gave me, how her face was mutilated by fists. "I'm sorry…"

She whimpered into the phone, releasing a quiet sniff. "Lizzie…"

"I'm sorry." I'd already said those words, but I needed to say them again. I really meant them. I would have saved her friend if I could have. I would have done anything to give Adelina what she wanted.

She started to cry.

"*Bellissima…*"

"I'm sorry," she whispered. "I always hoped I'd see her again..."

"She's in a better place now." After all the suffering she'd endured, being given the sweet release of death was exactly what she would have wanted. It was something I understood because I'd been in the same predicament before.

"I'll let you go, Cane." She stifled her tears so she could speak. "I know you've got your hands full right now."

I wanted to run back to Tuscany and comfort her the way she needed. But I had other obligations that prevented me from doing that. My brother was my priority. I had to make sure he was okay, make sure Pearl got to his side safely. "We'll talk about it when I get back."

"It's okay. There's nothing more to say..."

"But I want to be there for you, *Bellissima*..."

"I know you do."

Chapter 9

PEARL

Once the plane landed, the men escorted Lars and me into a series of three blacked-out SUVs. I felt like a high-class prisoner being transported from one place to the next. All the windows were tinted, and it was impossible to see inside the cars. The men still operated like I was a target for Tristan—even though he was long gone.

Even though Crow was nowhere nearby, I felt safe.

We hit the road and drove through Rome to the hospital where Crow was. Cane gave me an update an hour ago and said he was still in surgery. He hadn't heard any updates from the nurse or the doctor, which was a good thing. No news was good news.

Thirty minutes later, we pulled up to the circular entrance at the hospital, and the men helped me out.

Cane was there, dressed in all black. He had a cut above

his eyebrow and a few dirt stains, but he was in good shape. Until I looked at him, I didn't even realize that I'd never asked if he had been injured during the raid. "I can take it from here, guys." Cane took me by the elbow and pulled me away.

"Mr. Barsetti?"

We both turned around to see Lars getting out of the SUV, dressed in jeans and a t-shirt.

Cane nearly did a double take. "Lars? I didn't know you owned jeans."

Lars held his hands together in front of his waist, just as he did when he was working at the estate. "Would it be too intrusive if I came along? I know I serve Mr. Barsetti, but I've always viewed him like a son…"

My eyes immediately watered, and I grabbed his hand. "Of course, Lars. You are family."

Cane patted him on the back. "Crow will be happy to see you."

Cane guided us to the surgical floor and found us seats in the waiting room. A few other people were there, reading magazines or looking at their phones to keep busy. We sat down in the corner, but I couldn't stop shaking my leg. The anxiety was getting to me, making me desperate for air even though I was breathing normally.

Cane leaned forward and massaged his knuckles as he stared at the floor.

Lars sat with a straight and rigid back, still like a statue and soundless like the night.

The silence was killing me.

The passage of time was torture.

When I thought an hour had passed, it was only twenty minutes.

I reminded myself that the worst was over. Crow had been rescued, and Tristan was dead. All Crow had to do was make it through this surgery, and our lives would be back to normal. We could have the quiet life we'd always wanted…the three of us.

I just had to stay calm.

Be patient.

But after an actual hour passed and we didn't get an update, I started to worry again. "Cane, should we ask again? Do we talk to the front desk?"

Cane nodded to the nurse who sat behind the front desk. A phone was pressed to her ear as she spoke quietly so no one in the waiting room could hear her. "She's the one I've been asking. But I doubt she knows anything because she would have said something by now. I'll ask again if you want…"

"It's okay. I just wonder how long this surgery is."

"They had a lot to take care of, so it could be hours. It's been six already." Cane glanced at his watch.

Lars patted my hand. "He's going to be alright, Mrs. Barsetti. If he's made it this long, he's doing well."

"You think?" I whispered.

"Definitely."

We waited another hour, a very long and painful hour.

Finally, the nurse behind the desk walked up to Cane.

We all rose to our feet, but I stood up the quickest. "Is he okay?" I blurted.

"They just finished," she said. "Everything went well. They'll be transporting him to his room any minute now. He'll be out for a few more hours, so be patient."

Tears formed in my eyes as the relief swept over me. Crow made it through the most difficult part. I would see his face soon. I would finally get to hold his hand. I would finally get to be reunited with him.

"That's great," Cane said. "Thank you so much."

"I knew he would be alright," Lars said.

We returned to our seats, feeling a little better now that we'd received great news.

"Do you want to be in there alone?" Cane asked. "Until he wakes up?"

I wanted to wrap my arms around Crow and never let go. I wanted to tell him I loved him a million times and splash his skin with my tears. But I didn't care if Cane and Lars watched the whole thing. They were family. "No. He'll be happy to see all of us."

———

I CRIED when I first saw him.

His right eye was black and swollen, and there were scars all over his face. His abdomen was wrapped in gauze to protect his ribs, and he had a cast on his left leg. The doctor said he had several broken ribs that needed to be repaired, and the internal bleeding from a hernia had also been fixed.

Even though he would be alright, I was still heartbroken.

It was hard to look at him.

I wished Tristan weren't dead so I could kill him myself.

Cane didn't blink an eye over it. He'd seen his brother in worse condition when he pulled him out of that compound. Lars didn't show any emotion, but he never took his eyes off Crow's face.

We waited for Crow to wake up. Another four hours went by, and there was still no sign of movement. The sky had turned black as the night deepened and visiting hours were over, but that didn't have any effect on us. No amount of security would get us to leave his room.

After what seemed like an eternity, Crow took a deep breath, and his fingers curled into a fist. He didn't open his eyes right away, but his jaw clenched like he was having a bad dream. He suddenly opened his eyes and looked at the ceiling, his chest rising and falling hard as he switched into distressed mode. "Button...I need to call her." He didn't notice the three of us sitting there because he was still disoriented, unable to take in his surroundings even though his eyes were open.

I leaped from my seat and came to his side, grabbing his hand and being careful to avoid the IV. "Crow, I'm right here." My hand moved to his chest, and I slowly lowered him back onto the bed.

"Button." His hand grabbed mine, and he squeezed it before he locked his eyes on mine. It took him three full seconds to recognize me, to understand he was looking right into my face. His hand slowly released its grip, and he sighed under his breath. "I can't tell if I'm dreaming."

"The doctor said the anesthesia takes a little while to wear off, but you aren't dreaming. This is real. I'm right here." I interlocked our fingers and ran the fingers of my other hand through his hair. His right eye was still severely swollen, and I could barely make out his iris. His green eyes were dark, so they blended in with the purple discoloration and the irritated flesh.

The movements of his chest slowly returned to a normal pace, and he pulled me closer to him, his long arm moving around my waist as he positioned me. He turned his neck and pressed a kiss to my stomach before he rested his face there, right against my flat stomach.

My eyes watered and my chest ached. I could have lost my husband. This reality could have been completely different. He hardly said a word to me, but he showed his love for both of us with the sweetest touches. My finger stroked his hair, and I watched him close his eyes and lie there.

His lips moved against my shirt. "I can't wait to meet you…"

Tears dripped down my cheeks, and I withheld the sniffles that burned in my nose.

Crow turned his face and looked up at me, seeing the emotion etched into every feature of my face. "I'm alright, Button. Give me a few days, and I'll be back to new."

"It's gonna be more than a few days." Cane walked to the other side of the bed and rested his hand on Crow's shoulder.

Crow turned to him, a slight smile coming onto his lips. He was still slightly high, but with every minute, he was coming back to his regular self.

"At least a month," he said. "But that's what Lars is for."

Lars joined Cane's side and rested his hand on Crow's. "I'm so glad you're alright, Mr. Barsetti. Mrs. Barsetti and I were worried the entire time."

"Lars, call me Crow. We've known each other long enough to use first names."

Lars patted his hand. "I'll allow myself the luxury just for today. But tomorrow, it's back to Mr. Barsetti."

Crow chuckled. "Sounds fair." He turned back to Cane. "Everything go alright? How many did we lose?"

"Five," Cane answered.

"How about Bran?" Crow asked.

"He's fine. Got shot in the chest, but the vest protected him."

"Good," Crow said. "Bran is a good man. I'd miss him."

I smiled down at Crow, loving the way he was more affectionate than usual. Most of the time, he was brooding and quiet, shutting off all his feelings and pretending he didn't have any.

"He's dead, right?" Crow asked next.

"Yeah," Cane said. "I took care of it."

"You're certain?" Crow pressed.

"Yeah," Cane said. "Shot him between the eyes twice. Dumped his body in a landfill."

"Good," Crow whispered. "That's what he deserved."

I ran my hand up and down Crow's arm, massaging him so he wouldn't get worked up over Tristan, someone who was officially gone. "The doctor said you'll be here for a few days before they let you go."

"I want to go home now." Crow's broodiness started to rise. He wanted his way at all times—even when a health professional disagreed with him. "I miss Lars's cooking."

Lars smiled. "You didn't like the frozen lasagnas?"

"They were good," he said. "But not as good as when they're fresh. And I'm not eating hospital food...probably tastes like shit."

Cane chuckled. "I like you better like this."

"Strange," Crow said. "I think I like you better too."

Lars patted Cane on the back. "It's nice to see the two of you getting along. A very rare sight."

"I love my brother," Crow said bluntly. "Not sure why I never say it..."

My eyes softened, and I turned to Cane.

Cane couldn't hide the touched expression on his face.

"I love you too, man. I'm glad you aren't mad at me over this whole thing."

"How can I be mad?" Crow said quietly. "We went to hell and back for my wife. I'd do the same for yours."

Cane nodded, but he couldn't hide his look of pain, obviously thinking about the fact that Adelina said she didn't feel the same way.

Lars patted Cane on the shoulder. "Let's give these two some privacy."

Cane walked out with Lars, still wearing the sadness on his face.

Now that it was just the two of us, I pulled up a chair and took a seat at his bedside. My hand rested on his arm, and I treasured the feel of his warm skin. I traced the web of veins across the surface, remembering each one without even touching them.

Crow watched me, turning serious now that Lars and Cane were gone. His eyes were slightly different because of the drugs in his system, but he gave me that intense look I'd come to expect from him. It was a look he only gave me. No one else in the world had the luxury of receiving that scorching expression. "All I could think about was you and our little one…"

I smiled when I heard him talk that way about our baby like he was already a part of our lives. I hadn't known how Crow would react when I told him I was pregnant. He didn't seem enthused about having a family. But he was so supportive, even if that wasn't how he really felt. But now, he seemed genuinely excited. "I was afraid you wouldn't be happy when I told you I was pregnant..."

He didn't turn away from the comment. "I didn't want a family. It was the last thing on my mind. But the idea of you being pregnant with something we made together...is pretty incredible. And thinking about the two of you while I was in Tristan's captivity kept me going...kept me sane. It numbed the pain in a way medication never could." His hand moved over mine. "I didn't want our child to grow up never knowing me. I couldn't let that happen."

"And you didn't."

He brought my hand to his lips and kissed it. "I'm telling Cane I'm leaving the business. We're going to have a quiet life from now on. Just the two of us and wine. No more running. No more looking over our shoulders. I promise."

I realized Crow didn't know what Cane had sacrificed to save him. "Cane gave the business to the Skull Kings."

Crow took a little longer to grasp information than he usually did. Until the medication wore off completely, his thoughts would be convoluted. When his eyes dilated and his jaw tightened slightly, I knew he understood what I'd said to him. "He did? Why?"

"He couldn't round up enough men to save you. Everyone he called was too far away or there wasn't enough time. I suggested we make a trade with them. In exchange for their help, Cane had to hand over the business."

Crow's eyes softened as he sighed. He looked up at the

ceiling with one hand resting on his chest. His eyes shifted slightly back and forth as he thought to himself in silence.

My hand stayed on his. "That must have been hard for him."

"He knows it was worth it. There was no other option."

He turned his eyes back to me. "I guess that solves our problem, then."

"I'm excited. Maybe I'll finally be able to go shopping on my own now…"

The corner of his mouth rose in a smile. "Don't push it."

Chapter 10

CANE

I drove through the countryside and approached my house as dawn broke. I spent the evening at the hospital with Pearl and Lars. Pearl was exhausted from not sleeping much over the past few days, so I told her I would stay awake and look after Crow.

Even though he was fine.

When morning arrived, I headed back to my house outside Florence. The sun was rising above the horizon and sprinkling the fields with gold and green. Vineyards were everywhere, and the purple grapes looked deeper in color at this time of day. I pulled in front of the house and walked inside, knowing Adelina would still be asleep.

She was sitting on the couch when I walked inside, wearing one of my t-shirts and sporting messy hair. It seemed like she'd slept on the couch because there was a bunched-up blanket kicked to the side. "You're home..." She nearly jumped off the couch as she ran into my arms. She crashed into me and wrapped her arms around my waist. It was a greeting a woman gave to her man after being separated for a long period of time. It was affectionate, loving, and the way her face lit up when she saw me was priceless.

She gave me something worth coming home to.

"How's Crow doing? Is Pearl alright?"

"My brother is good. The surgery went well, and he's supposed to go home tomorrow. Pearl is with him."

"I'm glad they're reunited." Her cheek was pressed into my chest, so she turned her face so she could look up at me. "And I'm glad you're home too. That nightmare is finally over. We can both sleep well tonight knowing there's no one out there trying to get us."

"Yeah, it'll be a nice change." I angled my neck down and kissed her on the forehead. I didn't know why I did those sorts of things. I never saw Crow do it to Pearl, so I wasn't sure where the influence came from. "And I'm very sorry about Lizzie."

Her face immediately fell in sadness again. "It's not fair that I survived and she didn't."

"No, it's not. But she would be happy if she knew you escaped." My hands moved around her slender waist, and I felt the feminine curves I'd memorized. I loved her body, every feature, every touch. No other woman in the world stole my sexual attention the way Adelina did. She had the softest skin, the cutest freckles, the brightest eyes…everything about her was perfect. But her gorgeous features didn't do justice to the beauty underneath. Her light continued to shine even during her darkest times. She reminded me of Pearl in many ways, but she somehow seemed even stronger.

"I need to tell her family…to give them closure."

"Yeah, you should." Not knowing what happened was worse than hearing the painful truth.

"How did she…?" She didn't produce a coherent sentence, but she didn't need to. The question was clear.

"It doesn't matter. She's dead. That's it."

"Her parents are going to want to know."

"It's not going to lead to justice. I already killed Tristan and every man who worked for him. Whoever it was that hurt her is long gone. They've been punished. Knowing exactly what happened to her and how she was killed isn't going to lead to any new evidence. In this instance, less is more."

Adelina lowered her eyes, tucked her hair behind her ear, and nodded.

"Don't let this weigh you down. She'd be happy that you got away."

"I know she would."

"Then I hope you can find some peace…eventually." My hands moved to her cheeks, and I cupped her face. Her skin felt cold to the touch, her bright eyes seemed dark. My thumb brushed the corner of her mouth before I leaned in and kissed her. I missed the passion we used to have, the way I dove deep between her legs in my bed, but now I just wanted to touch her. I wanted to feel the connection between us. She didn't love me, but when my mouth was on hers, I could pretend that she did.

She kissed me back, her fingers wrapping around my wrists.

My kiss intensified even though I didn't do it intentionally. My mouth was working on its own, drunk off the way she made me feel. My life had been a roller coaster for the last three days. I hadn't slept. I hadn't felt good once. Her affection was the greatest drug I'd ever consumed.

I wanted to keep going, but I hadn't showered, and this couldn't go anywhere. Sometimes we fooled around, but I didn't expect her to be ready for sex. I wasn't an asshole, and I would never pressure her. When she was ready, she would tell me. I ended the embrace and stepped back. "I'm going to shower and get to bed. I'm pretty tired."

"Have you slept?"

I shook my head.

"You want me to make you something to eat?"

I was hungry, but I was too exhausted for food. "That's okay, but thank you." I dropped my hand and walked upstairs to the bedroom. The sheets were messy from the last time we'd slept together. I undressed and got into the shower, letting the warm water wash away all the grime under my fingertips. My hands smelled like the metal from my gun, and my hair was caked with dirt. I closed my eyes as I felt the refreshing sensation drip down my body. My brother was safe, Adelina was free, Pearl was happy… Everything was as it should be.

But I was still miserable.

Adelina and I hadn't spoken more about that awkward conversation we had over dinner. I'd brushed it off at the time, and I think I'd been believable. I wasn't going to be pathetic and let her see how much she hurt me—how much she devastated me. I wasn't sure where that left us now. She wasn't my prisoner anymore, and there was no one outside these four walls that wanted to hurt her.

She was free.

But what would she do with that freedom?

Would she choose to spend it with me?

The glass door opened, and Adelina walked inside with her gorgeous nakedness. Her beautiful nipples were firm because of the cold in the bathroom. She stepped under the water with me, and her hair was immediately soaked until it clung to the back of her neck. She looked at me for an invitation even though she didn't need one.

My eyes roamed over her body, seeing the faint hints of bruises that still marked her skin. The worst of it had passed, but the more serious injuries still needed time to heal. When I looked at her skin, I didn't think of the places where Tristan had touched her. I didn't think she was infected, broken.

I saw the same woman I saw before.

I wanted to treasure her beautiful body like it'd never

been touched at all. I wanted to erase every memory she had of Tristan. I wanted to make sex beautiful and pleasurable. I'd shown that to her once before, but I could do it again until the message sank in.

She stepped under the shower and looked up at me as the water fell down her face. Her hands moved up my chest, exploring the hard muscles underneath her fingertips. She studied me like a mountain climber looking for the perfect grip. "I know you're tired. I just miss you."

My hands moved to her hips, and I pressed my forehead to hers. If I could do whatever I wanted, I would lift her up and make love to her right then and there. But until I got her permission, I couldn't do whatever I pleased. "I don't want you to miss me. So stay until you don't."

Chapter 11

CROW

The medication masked the pain, but I felt weaker than I ever had. My ribs would take time to heal, my leg needed time to regain its strength, my eye was still swollen and purple. If I shifted my body a certain way, my stomach hurt. There were stitches along my abdomen, and I had to make sure I didn't tear them by moving too quickly.

I hated feeling this way.

I hated feeling so weak.

My family wasn't in danger, but I liked to be prepared for any eventuality. A hard life had taught me to be ready for anything—especially the unexpected.

The doctor said I was free to go and offered me a wheelchair.

Fuck that. "I'll walk."

"You shouldn't put any weight on that leg for at least

two more days," the nurse said as he engaged the brakes on the wheels.

"I can walk," I repeated.

Button rolled her eyes. "I'm sorry. He's very stubborn…"

I rose to my feet in a new pair of clothes Lars had retrieved for me. I wore dark jeans and a black t-shirt, the typical stuff I wore around the house. I felt like myself, but my body wasn't quite the same. I still felt pain from my left leg, but I didn't show the grimace on my face. "I'm fine. Let's go."

Button gave me a pissed look and pointed to the chair. "Sit down, or I'll make you."

I didn't question the fiery look she gave me. I knew she meant business. She might be half my size, but she could do some serious damage if she wanted. Without raising a fist, she could make me feel like shit with just her words. She was pregnant and terrified for my well-being, so I sucked it up and obeyed.

The nurse winked at her.

———

THE BOTTOM WINDOWS of the house had been repaired. Lars must have taken care of the arrangements, swept up the broken glass, and fixed the window behind the kitchen. It didn't seem like anyone had been there to kill me.

I walked into the house at a slower pace than I usually moved, but I held myself as straight as ever. All of my bones could be broken, but I'd still find a way to walk like a man.

Lars emerged from the kitchen, back in his tuxedo. "Mr. Barsetti, it's nice to have you back."

"It's nice to be back."

He stood with his hands behind his back, staring at me with a discreet look of fondness. "Would you like me to prepare lunch? I know you weren't a fan of the hospital food." He smiled, teasing me for the slipup I'd had when I was still a little high.

"Lunch would be great, Lars."

"Perfect. I'll bring it to your bedroom."

"I'll take it in the dining room."

"No." Button's aggressive voice came from behind me. "You're getting into bed, and you're staying there until I say otherwise."

I was so happy to be reunited with my wife, but she was such a major pain in the ass. "I'm not sick."

"But you aren't well either." She turned to Lars. "He'll take lunch upstairs. I'm gonna get him in the shower first."

"I can shower on my own," I snapped. "I'm not helpless."

"You don't want to shower with a beautiful, naked woman?" she asked incredulously.

My eyes narrowed on her face. "When you put it that way…"

"Thank you, Lars." Button grabbed my hand and guided me to the stairs.

"It's nice to have you back, Your Grace." Lars gave a swift bow before he walked into the kitchen.

It took me longer than normal to get up the stairs. There were times when I wanted to take a break, but I refused to show weakness in front of Button. I wasn't trying to protect her, just to show her that nothing could slow me down. I was still the protector I'd always been.

We got into the bedroom, and she started the water. She stripped all of her clothes off then returned to me. She pulled my shirt over my head then worked my jeans.

My eyes were on her tits.

It didn't matter what we were doing. If her top was off, I thought about sex.

By the time my jeans and boxers were off, I was already hard.

She smiled as she looked at it. "Looks like everything is still working properly."

"Maybe you should make sure."

I LAY IN BED, bandaged up and exhausted. I had just taken more pain killers to control the throbbing sensation all over my body. My ribs hurt the most. Just taking a breath was painful. A fire was burning in the hearth, and the sun was beginning to set.

Button sat beside me in bed wearing one of my t-shirts. Her brown hair was pulled over one shoulder, and her face was free of makeup. She hadn't put any on since she showered, but I preferred her appearance this way. She wasn't hiding behind anything. It was nothing but her, in her purest form.

She scooted close to my side and kissed my shoulder. She was careful to snuggle with me without touching my injured areas. She normally rubbed my chest, but that area was off-limits because it was too close to my ribs.

I stared at her beside me, treasuring the sight of her face. I'd pictured it constantly to keep my strength. It was strange to think there was a time in my life when I wasn't living for her, when she wasn't the motivation behind everything I did. My life didn't seem that valuable until she walked through the door. Now, I lived every day for her, to make sure I would be alive to make her days perfect.

And now, I had another person to live for—someone I hadn't met. "Does it feel different?"

"What?" she whispered.

My hand moved to her flat stomach, my large fingers stretching across her entire torso. It wasn't that I had big hands, but she was particularly petite. "To be pregnant."

"In the beginning, it was. I felt sick pretty often."

"And what about now?"

"I don't know." She placed her hand on top of mine. "I guess I don't feel different. I guess I don't look different. But knowing they're in there…that feels different. I don't know if it's a boy or a girl, but I can feel them. I don't feel like the only person in this body."

My hand pulled up her shirt, and my fingertips felt her bare skin. There was no way to detect someone was deep inside. She'd only been pregnant for weeks. It would take months before we noticed a change in her body. "When I'm better, you can expect me to wait on you hand and foot. I'll get you all the ice cream you want, make you as many fires as you want…"

"You already do those things." She smiled at me, her affection obvious.

"Then you don't have to feel as bad for asking me to do it."

"I never ask, Crow."

I did those things on my own, making sure she had what she needed. I never thought I'd be a good person to take care of another human being, but the second Button became mine, I automatically did everything for her. Sometimes I was cold and distant, but she was still the first person in my life. "I guess I spoil you too much."

"You do." She moved closer into my body and pressed a kiss to the corner of my mouth.

My arm circled her waist, and I pulled her tighter to me, hugging her even though it made me wince in pain. The discomfort was worth the pleasure. I kissed her back and sucked her bottom lip into my mouth. I wasn't a man of many words, and the best way I communicated with Button was by touch. I wanted to make love to her, to erase the hardship we'd both experienced. But I was too weak, and she would never allow it to happen.

So I kissed her instead.

The kisses turned hotter, deeper. I felt the connection deep down inside me, the burning need to take more of her. I could have died in that warehouse, but I was here with her now. I was kissing my wife as our baby grew inside her.

She pulled away first, probably because we were getting carried away. She licked her lips, tasting me one last time before she shifted back. "What do you think we'll have?"

I hadn't given it much thought. "I don't know. I don't care."

"Really?" She cocked her head to the side, examining me with intelligent eyes. "You don't prefer a son?"

"Why would I?"

"Every man wants a son."

Just a month ago, I wasn't thinking about having a family at all. It was a luxury I didn't care about. I imagined our lives would be just about the two of us. So I never thought about my preferences. "As long as they're healthy, I'll be happy."

She smiled.

"Do you want a boy or a girl?" If I had a son, I imagined he'd look a lot like me. I would raise him to be similar, to inherit my strengths and avoid my weaknesses. If I had a daughter, I imagined she would look just like Button. She'd be beautiful, with thick brown hair and gorgeous eyes.

She'd inherit her mother's love of life and also her ferocity. When she grew older, a man would fall in love with her— and I'd have to kill him.

"I don't know…"

"I retract my statement. I want a boy."

"Really?" she asked. "Why?"

"If we had a daughter, she'd be beautiful like you…and I'd never let her leave the house."

She chuckled. "You never let me leave the house, so I believe you."

"A boy would be easier."

"Even if we have a boy now, we could have a girl later."

"We're having more kids?" I asked in surprise. "How about we focus on this one for right now?"

"We can't have just one."

I didn't mind knocking her up, but I wasn't sure if I wanted the outcome. "How many are we talking here?"

"How many are you willing to go for?"

Both of my eyebrows rose.

"How about four?" she suggested.

Jesus Christ. "You want four kids?"

"Yes."

"Four?" I repeated.

She chuckled. "Yes, Crow. I want four."

My parents only had three, and they felt overwhelmed most of the time. "Any reason why?"

"I want a family. I was in foster care, and then I was by myself… I've always been alone. There's not a single person on this earth who shares my DNA. You have Cane, but I don't have anyone."

I'd never thought of that before. I did have a special bond with someone that couldn't be severed. It didn't matter how much he pissed me off. He was my brother—and I always had his back because of it.

"So I want to make my own family. I want to hear their voices in the hallways. When they're adults, I want to have them in this beautiful home for every holiday."

I would give my wife anything, but I wasn't sure if I could give her that. "Let's start with two and see how it goes…"

She smiled at my compromise. "Thank you."

My hand moved into her hair, and I treasured the feeling of her soft skin. She was the perfect addition to this bed, the perfect complement to my life. Other women had slept where she slept, but they never left their ghost behind. I hadn't taken Button into the playroom since we'd been married because I had no urge. What we had was more than enough. "I can't wait until I'm back on my feet."

"I know lying around all day is going to be hard for you."

I got another chance at life, and my wife was already glowing with the life growing inside her. I didn't want to lie in this bed all day, my injuries wrapped up and healing. I wanted to make love to my wife—over and over.

I SAT up in bed and looked out the windows that led to the patio. It was a warm day despite the winter chill. The sun was shining, and the vineyards were vibrantly green. There was work building up on my desk at the vineyards, but I was unable to attend to it. Without having a purpose, I felt lazy.

It made me want to drink.

I couldn't have alcohol with my medication, so I had to skip the scotch. I was drinking a lot of water, and I never realized just how bland it was until I had to consume a lot of it. I was getting my meals in bed, and Button was tending to me like a nurse. She didn't seem to mind, but it made me feel emasculated.

Button walked through the door, her hair pulled back into a sleek ponytail. It showed the contours of her face, the beautiful slenderness of her neck. "You've got company."

"I don't have any friends."

Her mouth smiled, but her eyes narrowed. "Not true. Cane and Adelina are in the hallway. Can I bring them in?"

I was bored out of my mind, so why not? "Sure."

She grabbed a shirt from a drawer and tossed it at me. "Put this on."

I caught it and couldn't wipe the grin off my face.

"What?" she asked as she placed her hands on her hips.

"You don't want Adelina to see me shirtless. You really are a Barsetti." I pulled it on and leaned back against the headboard.

She strutted out of the room, her ass shaking in skintight jeans.

Damn, I couldn't wait until I could move again.

Button returned with Cane and Adelina. Cane was dressed like he was heading to work even though there was no longer a business to run. He wore all black with a leather jacket, and a pistol sat in the holster at his hip. Adelina was in black jeans and a gray sweater. She looked a lot better than the last time I saw her. Her face was free of bruises, and she wore a smile instead of a tearful face.

Cane walked to my side of the bed and looked down at me. "Still being lazy, huh?"

I didn't rise to the insult because I knew it was a joke. "Unfortunately."

"You look good, though." He clapped me on the shoulder, showing me more affection than he usually would. "Your eye looks a lot better. Don't look like a pirate anymore."

"When my ribs are healed, I'm kicking your ass for that."

Cane chuckled. "Good. I miss it." He stuck both of his hands in his pockets. "Seriously, how are you doing?"

"I've been better, but I've also been worse. I've got a beautiful wife to take care of me, so I shouldn't complain."

"And a butler," Cane added. "Who makes bomb-ass food."

I chuckled. "Yeah, he does."

Adelina came to my side next, her long, brown hair framed around her face. Her hand moved to mine on the bed, and she touched me in a way only a select few were allowed to touch me. When she'd hugged me a few weeks ago, I'd felt awkward as hell. It was strange to hug a woman besides my wife. But since she might be my sister-in-law soon, I'd have to let her in. "Thank you for everything that you did. I don't think I'll ever be able to repay you."

"You're welcome, Adelina. I'm happy you're free. Not all women are as lucky as you and Pearl."

"I know…" Her eyes immediately fell in sadness.

And I knew why. I hadn't thought about her friend until I was already done talking.

"I'm here if you ever need anything. I'm indebted to you for the rest of my life," she said. "If there's anything you ever want, please don't hesitate to ask. I'll make it happen if it's possible."

Our hands were still touching, and her fingers felt distinctly different from Pearl's. "You don't owe me anything, Adelina. You deserved to be free. Every person in this world deserves that luxury."

She gave a slight nod, her eyes full of emotion.

"But if you're insistent on doing something for me, I'm sure Pearl could use some help when the baby comes."

Her eyes fell again, but she quickly covered it up with a smile. "Of course. Anything she needs." She pulled her hand away and stepped back, moving behind Cane so it was just the two of us again.

He stared at me, a different expression on his face.

Pearl picked up on the tension and touched Adelina on

the elbow. "Let's give them some privacy." The girls walked out and shut the door behind them.

I adjusted myself on the bed and sat a little higher than last time.

Cane looked at my nightstand, where a picture of Button sat in a small frame.

"Pearl told me you traded the business for Constantine's help."

He stared at the picture a moment longer then nodded. "Yeah…I did." He turned back to me, the regret in his eyes. "I had to."

"I know that was hard for you."

"It was," he said honestly. "But there was no other option. I didn't have any more time. It was Pearl's idea, actually. And it was a good idea."

"How is it going to work, then?"

"They took everything. They took everything in the warehouses, the clients, and they hired all of our men to work for them. The second the job was done, they took the keys. You and I have no ownership over the place anymore."

It was so sudden. The transfer of power happened instantly. Constantine didn't want to wait, even after going into battle. "I'm sorry. I know it meant a lot to you."

"Yeah, it did," he said with a sigh. "But you mean a lot more."

Cane and I didn't exchange thoughts and feelings like the girls did. We stuck to business and insults. But now the emotion built up in the room between us. I could feel it from him, and he could feel it from me. Anytime my brother needed anything, I was there. I didn't do it out of obligation; I did it because he was one of the most important people to me. And he did the same for me. We had a bond that couldn't be severed by bullets or knives. It was concrete—and permanent. "Thank you."

"You don't need to thank me," he said quietly. "I would do it again in a heartbeat."

"I know. Just as I would have risked my life for the woman you loved again."

He shifted his gaze away, looking at a different spot on the wall. "I do love her. But she doesn't love me."

I studied his face and saw the hurt etched into his expression. He wasn't just hurt, but devastated. It was painful to say the words out loud, to admit the truth to me. He'd asked me to risk my life for a woman who would never be his wife.

"I didn't know that before I asked for your help…"

"What happened?" When Pearl came into the picture, Cane pestered me about my feelings all the time. He insisted I loved her, that I couldn't live without the woman. It was the first time we talked about romance. Now, exchanging feelings seemed to be the norm for us.

"Nothing really," he said with a sigh. "We were having dinner, and I told her. I looked her in the eye and said I loved her. She grew uncomfortable, got really quiet, and said nothing in response. I didn't want to make the situation worse, so I told her it was fine. Not a big deal." He still didn't look at me, avoiding eye contact.

"I'm sorry."

"Yeah…"

"But I said the same thing to Pearl, and it was bullshit."

"We aren't you," he said.

"That woman has been by your side for a few months. She enjoys being with you, enjoys spending time with Pearl. I wouldn't give up on her, Cane. The poor girl was taken from her home and yanked down into hell. It would be hard to justify loving a man who ever did business with Tristan to begin with, one who took her as a loan for a business deal. She just needs some time to work through those details."

"I risked my life to save her. Some of my men died. I put your life on the line… I put Pearl's on the line." He shook his head as he clenched his jaw. "She knew I loved her. She had to. But she just used me…"

I didn't know what to say to that. It was probably true. "Even if that's the case, she was just trying to survive. You can't blame her for that. You can't blame anyone for that. And if she really wanted to use you, she would have lied and said she loved you and asked you to keep her in the first place."

Cane crossed his arms over his chest. "Yeah…I guess that's true."

"I wouldn't give up on her just yet. You remember how long it took for me to admit I loved Pearl. I always knew I did, but I had to fight my own issues before I could allow myself to really feel it. Adelina has been through a lot, more than either of us could possibly understand." I'd always been a predator, as had Cane. We didn't know what it was like to be the subject of a cruel fantasy. No one ever wanted to use us for their own vile interests. With Pearl, I was the predator, and she was the prey. But our relationship worked because we both wanted it to be that way. She wanted me to be overbearing, protective, and obsessed.

"I realize that. I have compassion."

"Then be patient a little longer. Not all hope is lost."

"Maybe," he said noncommittally.

I rested back against the headboard and felt the pain in my ribs. It went down little by little every single day, but I still had a long way to go. My mind wanted me to be back on my feet, running in the morning and heading to work. But my broken body was stationary, needing the patience to regain its strength. It was such a pain in the ass. "Let's make wine together."

Cane grabbed a chair from the sitting area and pulled it up to my bedside. "Wine, huh?"

"Yeah."

"I'm surprised you aren't drinking scotch right now." He sat back and rested his knees far apart.

"I would if I could." I nodded to the door. "Mrs. Barsetti won't allow it."

"And we both know she runs the show," he teased.

I glared at him. "You want a job or not?"

"Crow, I don't know shit about wine. I don't even drink the piss."

"You can learn to love it."

"Doubtful. Besides, it seems pretty quiet over there. Not much for me to do anyway. And if you think I'm gonna haul boxes or drive shipping trucks, you're mistaken. Plus, I'm terrible with people, so I shouldn't have any direct contact with your clients."

"What a great resume…"

He rolled his eyes. "I'm just being honest, Crow. I have more than enough wealth to retire with a happy lifestyle. But I'm too young to retire. I'll go crazy sitting at home all day. Even with Adelina there, I need something more."

"I was thinking of expanding the business anyway. We could buy more land, and we could start up another winery. It could be private property so you wouldn't have to deal with clients. You could just oversee the harvesting, packaging, and distribution. You'd work in an office like I do. You would have the independence of working on your own without having to deal with me every day, but we would also be partners."

"So I'd take half of the profits from this new place?"

"You'd take half of everything, Cane."

He stared at me blankly. "What? You'd give me half of the winery you already built from the ground up?"

"Yeah. We're a team. It's not any different from the weapons business."

"That's a lot of dough, Crow."

I shrugged. "I have more than enough. I've been shoving money into different offshore accounts to hide it. I've invested in a lot of real estate because I don't know where to put it. Money isn't important to me anymore."

"Even with a kid on the way?"

"My wife and child will have more than enough when I'm gone. I don't need to worry about that." I'd already set up everything for her when my life was in danger. She knew exactly how to access the funds and live an extremely comfortable life. She could start over somewhere new if she wished. Or she could stay in the beautiful house I left for her. She didn't owe anyone anything, and she would be a very wealthy woman.

"You're sure?"

My brother sacrificed his business, the one thing that connected us to our father, so I could get out of there alive. Our relationship had always been about sacrifice, doing what we didn't want to do for each other. That was how family worked. I enjoyed running the business as my own, having my own space, but being partners with my brother wasn't the worst thing in the world. With the weapons business, we always got along...until he'd traded Adelina for weapons without my permission. "I'm sure. Just don't trade shipments of wine for women."

He rolled his eyes. "There's only one woman I would do that for, and I already have her."

"Then we won't have any problems." I extended my hand.

He took it. "Partners again…"

"And wine doesn't taste like piss."

"Your wine does."

My eyes narrowed.

"Kidding. I'll get used to it. I'll ask Pearl to give me a special wine tasting. I'll just drink some scotch in between."

"Wine tastes better when it's paired with food. I'll show you what I mean."

"Alright." He sat back in the chair and rested his arms on the armrests. "How long are you going to be like this?"

"A few weeks…at the minimum."

"That sucks."

"I hate it. And Pearl doesn't want me to lift a finger."

"That's not so bad. Is there anything I can do? Pearl might be able to give me a rundown on the winery, and I can go take care of a few things."

"No, it's okay. I can work from home…once she lets me."

"Alright. I'm here if you change your mind."

"I know."

He continued to sit there even though the conversation seemed to be over. "Got any names picked out?"

"Excuse me?"

"For the kid."

It hadn't crossed my mind. "No. We've got nine months to figure it out."

"I can't believe I'm gonna be an uncle. Never thought that would happen after Vanessa died."

"You think I'll be an uncle someday?" I asked.

Cane's expression hardened again. "Unlikely. Adelina is the only woman I've ever cared about, and she doesn't feel the same way. So…I doubt she wants to have my kid."

"So you want to have kids?"

He shrugged. "Before her, not really. With her…doesn't sound so bad."

I couldn't believe my brother and I were engaging in a conversation about kids. We went from being the biggest arms dealers in the country to being two men who talked about their women. When did so much change?

"Is Pearl giving you lots of blow jobs?"

I narrowed my eyes on his face, threatening him with a single look. I didn't talk about my wife in that context with anyone—especially not my brother. He'd wanted to fuck her once upon a time.

He chuckled and rose to his feet. "I'll let myself out."

Chapter 12

ADELINA

Cane drove us back to his house a few miles away. He lived fairly close to his brother, no longer than a fifteen-minute drive. Their proximity was obviously not a coincidence. The men talked shit to each other constantly, but underneath those words were their true feelings. They didn't like being farther apart than necessary, just far enough to have some privacy.

I was glad Cane returned whole, not scarred and injured the way Crow was. But our relationship hadn't been the same since that dinner we had. He was distant with me. He paid attention to me, kissed me when he wanted, and his eyes were on me most of the time. But now his thoughts were unknown.

We didn't talk the way we used to.

He brushed off my silence and said it was okay that I didn't feel the same way.

But I think I hurt him.

I'd never expected him to say those words to me. Cane didn't seem like the kind of man capable of emotions like that. While he was good, sweet, and wonderful, he said he'd never had a serious woman in his life. All he cared about was money, power, and sex. We were close and shared experiences no one else could possibly understand, but I thought that was the extent of it.

Besides, he was a criminal.

He did business with bad men and lived outside the law. I thought that he possessed a small ounce of compassion for me because he knew I deserved better, that he saved me because he'd become a better man.

I didn't know it was because he loved me.

We returned to the house and walked inside. Cane opened the fridge, grabbed a few things, and set them on the counter.

"Can I help?" It was the first time we'd spoken to each other in several hours.

He grabbed the cutting board and placed the carrots on top. "Sure. Wash and slice these."

"Okay." I ran them under warm water while Cane prepared the beef and onions. He was making beef stew inside one of the big silver pots on his stove.

"I'm hiring a butler this week. I offered Lars a ton of money, but he turned me down."

"I think it's because he loves Pearl." I patted the carrots dry then cut them into thin slices. "Can't put a price on that."

His back was to me. "Yeah, you're probably right. I'll find someone else. There're a lot of talented chefs around here." He placed everything inside then grabbed the carrots I prepared. He tossed those inside too then set the lid on top. "That'll be ready in a few hours." He exited the kitchen and entered the living room. "I'm gonna shower." Before I could catch up to him again, he was gone.

I didn't like the wall between us.

I didn't like the way he pushed me away.

We seemed to be going back in time, to when we hardly knew each other.

But I knew him now.

———

WE HAD dinner at the table, but Cane didn't look at me. His eyes were focused on his food or the view outside the window. It was dark because the sun was gone so there wasn't much to see, but he preferred to look at the land-scape instead of me.

There was no intimacy anymore.

We hadn't had sex since I returned from Tristan's because I needed more time. Now I was properly healed. The scars over my heart and behind my eyelids would be there forever, but I didn't think about them when Cane was with me. I didn't feel like a victim at all—only a survivor. Maybe if we were together again, we could have that connection I missed. Or maybe he would stay distant anyway. "I feel so bad for Crow. He looks terrible."

"You should have seen him a few days ago." Cane opened a bottle of wine and poured a glass. After taking a sniff, he took a drink. His jaw tensed, and his eyes narrowed in repulsion before he set it down again.

"You don't like red wine?"

"I don't like wine—period."

"Then why are you drinking it?"

"Crow and I are going to be partners in his wine business, so I'm going to have to force myself to like it."

"That's exciting. When is that going to start?"

"When he's back on his feet. He'll need at least a few weeks."

"Pearl seems like she's doing well."

"She's just happy he's home and alive. I know he looks bad, but that's nothing he can't get over. If she'd let him, he'd probably be moving around the house and going to work."

"Doesn't like to sit still?"

"No. Neither of us does."

"I picked up on that." I grabbed the bottle and poured myself a glass. I swirled it around before I took a sip. I was expecting something dry and bland based on his reaction, but it was sultry and smooth. "This is good."

"You have better taste than I do."

"Wine is an acquired taste. It can be bold and delicious. It'll take some time to get used to. I know you prefer strong liquor."

"Crow does too, but he seems to like it."

"Give it time."

Cane still hadn't looked at me. I knew it wasn't because of my captivity with Tristan. It was because of the divider he placed between us, the barrier that was present day and night.

I didn't like this. "Cane?"

"Hmm?" He took another bite of food, his eyes down.

I lost my appetite even though I hadn't eaten much that day. "We need to talk about this…"

"Talk about what?" He raised his head and looked me in the eye—for the first time that evening. His eyes were devoid of emotion, and he seemed indifferent, as if he was really over that awkward conversation we had.

"You know what I'm talking about."

"You'll need to spell it out for me, sweetheart. I can't read your mind…as I learned the hard way."

Sweetheart? Can't read my mind? "I know things have been different between us because of that dinner we had." I didn't need to specify further than that. I was certain we were both on the same page. "I don't want it to be this way."

"That makes no sense." He dropped his fork onto the

plate. "Because this is exactly how you want it to be. You don't love me, and that's fine. This is how two people act when they don't love each other. You expect me to kiss the ground you walk on? I already risked my life and my brother's life to save you. I've given you enough, and I'm not giving you any more." He left the table and abandoned his food. "You can't have it both ways, Adelina. I'm not some idiot stuck under your thumb." He stormed out of the kitchen, his rage filling every inch of the room.

"Cane."

He didn't stop.

I went after him and caught up to him in the living room. "It's not like that, Cane."

"You used me." He turned around, his thick arms shaking by his sides. "You used me, and you know it."

"No, I didn't. You know I would never do something like that."

He shook his head, his eyes fierce.

"I really care about you——"

"Shut up."

My eyes widened at the slap he'd just landed with his words.

"I don't want to hear how much you care about me. I don't want to hear you call me your friend. It's insulting. Anything you say that doesn't match what I say is just annoying. So just don't say anything at all." He looked at me with the same glare he showed Tristan. It seemed like he wanted to wrap his large hands around my neck and strangle me until I was no longer on this earth.

"I don't want it to be this way."

"Then don't talk about it. Problem solved."

"We need to talk about it. It obviously bothers you—"

"I'm fine, Adelina. You meant nothing to me once upon a time. You'll mean nothing to me again."

———

CANE IGNORED me for the next few days.

We slept in the same bed the way we did before, but that was because I refused to sleep anywhere else. I'd be lying if I said I was completely okay after what happened, and sleeping next to Cane made me feel safe. Tristan was dead, and there was no one out there to get me, but listening to him breathe as I fell asleep was the most comforting thing in the world.

I spent my time watching TV and reading. He spent his time working out, running errands, and maintaining the yard outside. He interviewed a few people for the butler position—all men.

One afternoon, he grabbed his wallet and keys and prepared to leave.

"Where are you going?"

He gave me a dark look that told me I shouldn't have asked.

"If you're going to see Crow, I'd like to come."

After a long pause, he nodded. "Then let's go."

We got into the car together and drove across the fields to his brother's house. Instead of letting the silence linger in the car, Cane turned on the radio and had it at a volume louder than necessary, just to make sure I understood he had no interest in speaking to me.

Message received.

We arrived at the house, and Lars greeted us. He wasn't as friendly to Cane as he was to Pearl and me. I wasn't sure what caused the slight tension between them, but I knew Cane wouldn't tell me if I asked—not anymore.

Pearl came downstairs and greeted us in the entryway. "Here to check on your brother?" Pearl hugged Cane hard before she stepped back.

"Yeah," Cane answered. "How's he doing?"

"He's getting better every single day." She hugged me next. "He's been moody staying in bed constantly, and his sourness is aggravating sometimes."

"Maybe a blow job wouldn't hurt," Cane advised with a smile.

"I'm not gonna tell Crow you said that because he'd come down here and kick your ass." She placed her hands on her hips but spoke with a smile. "But he's been getting plenty of those, not that it's any of your business."

"Then you must be doing it wrong because he wouldn't be so pissed if you were doing it right," Cane teased.

Pearl smacked him on the arm. "Maybe I will tell him."

"He's looking for an excuse to punch me anyway."

Cane made his way to the stairs and went up to the third floor where Crow's bedroom was located.

Pearl turned back to me, wearing dark jeans and a black t-shirt. She didn't seem pregnant at all, but in a few months, her belly would finally start to show. "You're welcome to go up and say hi as well. But I'm sure the men want to speak alone for a bit. They tend to do that…be secretive."

"Yeah, I picked up on that."

"You want to come outside with me and help me with the garden? The flowers that were destroyed had to be replaced because they couldn't recover from the tires and glass."

"Yeah, sure."

We went outside together, pulled on some gloves, and dug into the earth.

"Crow is doing well?" I asked.

"Yeah. The doctor came by to check on him, and he said Crow's in great shape. He just needs to be more patient and let everything heal. His leg seems to be better, but I want him to rest in bed a little longer."

"Sounds good to me."

"I need him to heal correctly, because when I'm seven months into my pregnancy, I'm gonna need a strong man to help me out." When she talked about the baby, she possessed an undeniable glow. Her smile was infectious, and joy twinkled in her eyes like Christmas lights.

"You're excited, huh?"

"I wasn't ready to have a baby immediately, but now that it's coming, it feels right."

"How many do you want to have?"

"Crow thinks we're going to have two, but we're going to have four."

I chuckled. "He's in for a surprise."

"Once the first two arrive, he'll realize we need more."

"You're probably right."

She dug the dirt out of the hole in the earth and set it into the pail at our side. "How are you doing, Adelina? Everything alright?"

"I know the trauma is supposed to hit me now that it's over, but I'm just so relieved to be free. Right now, I feel good. I feel lucky. The only thing that really hurts is Lizzie. I wish she were here with me now…"

"I'm sorry, Adelina. I wish we could have saved your friend."

"Me too. But Cane told me she would be happy that I escaped. I know he's right…"

"He is right. When I was free from Bones and in Crow's captivity, I never had a breakdown. I never had that moment where everything came crashing down. I think being with Crow was therapy for me. He told me I wasn't a victim, but a survivor. He said he never saw me as a woman who was raped. He never thought about any man before him because he erased them. I guess he gave me a clean start…wouldn't let me feel sorry for myself."

Cane did the same thing to me.

"I know they've both been through a lot, and that's made them into the strong men they are today. I guess they expect us to be the same way."

"Not a bad way to live." I could sit around and feel sorry for myself, or I could be grateful I got to feel the sunlight on my face again.

Pearl grabbed the small rosebush and placed it in the ground where the dead plant had been before. She used her hands to compact the dirt into place, not pushing down too hard so water could still drip through. "Cane mentioned your conversation…"

I was surprised he'd told her. It seemed like something he might mention to his brother, but not to anyone else.

She smoothed out the surface then turned to me. "He wouldn't want me to tell you this, but he was pretty hurt by it."

"I know."

"I guess he was expecting a different response from you." She sat back on her knees and looked at me. There wasn't disappointment or accusation in the look. She wasn't judgmental like someone else might be. "You had nothing but good things to say about him, so I guess I'm surprised too."

"Because I think he's a good man. Of course I have nothing but nice things to say about him."

"It seemed like more than that."

"It is more than that," I whispered. "Cane is important to me. When he went to save Crow, I was worried about him the entire time. He's the reason I haven't lost my sanity. Ever since I came into his home, he's made me feel like a person and not a piece of property. I don't see him as just a friend because I like being with him. But, love…? I don't know about that. I've never loved a man before, but I imagined it would be very different from this."

She got comfortable on the blanket and pulled off her gardening gloves. "How so?"

"I didn't have any experience before Tristan took me. I'd always been waiting for the right guy. I'd seen all my friends date jerks and get their hearts broken. I didn't want to deal with all of that. I wanted to find the one and just be happy. So I figured I would meet him at work or in a coffee shop…he'd ask me on a date to the movies or something. It would be simple but spectacular. With Cane…it's been nothing like that. He accepted me as a loan from another criminal he was doing business with. If I didn't sleep with him, he was going to return me to Tristan. It's not how I imagined falling in love."

Pearl watched me closely, her eyes hiding her opinion. "Nothing ever goes the way we plan, Adelina."

"I know."

"I didn't expect to fall in love with Crow. For a long time, I viewed him as a barbaric criminal. The only reason I considered myself lucky to be with him was because he wasn't cruel like the other men I'd met. But as time passed, I realized he was the best person for me. The terms we met under weren't great. Our relationship didn't start off with a coffee date. But if I'd returned to America permanently and found someone else, they never would have been able to give me what I needed. I fell in love with Crow because I was meant to fall in love with him. Our relationship isn't perfect—but it works for us."

I could feel her love for him when she spoke. There was no doubt in her mind that she'd made the right decision. She left behind her entire life in America to live in Tuscany with a man who once owned her.

"I think your feelings for Cane are stronger than you realize. Maybe you just need a little more time to figure it out."

"Maybe...but he's angry with me."

"He's only angry because he loves you," she whispered. "And he just wants you to love him in return."

"I don't know if I can do that..."

"You don't have to force yourself to. You just have to not force yourself not to."

"He's a criminal, Pearl. I don't think my parents would be thrilled with my choice of a partner. They'd make me see a psychiatrist."

"No one in the world will ever understand what you went through besides you," she said quietly. "So don't listen to what other people think. Let them think you're crazy. Doesn't matter."

"I'm just not sure if he's what I want," I whispered. "Like I said, I want a different kind of relationship."

She looked at the ground for a moment before she

looked up again. "Nobody is perfect. We all have skeletons in our closets. Cane is just more transparent about his than the rest of us."

"He told me how he hurt you…"

"And he would never do something like that again—to anyone. He's a much different man now than the one I first met. You've seen his transition yourself. He's not even the same man as when you first laid eyes on him. When I returned to America and tried to get my life back together, I started seeing an old boyfriend. He was good, handsome, clean…everything I would have wanted in a boyfriend once upon a time. But it didn't work. It didn't fit. Every time I slept with him, all I could think about was Crow. He left a mark on me that I could never erase. I saw him as a dark and twisted man, but I realized I had become just as dark and twisted. Nothing could change that. That was how I was—forever. And that's when I knew where I belonged."

———

CANE UNDRESSED himself and left his pile of clothes on the floor. His ass was tight in his boxers, and his hard physique was chiseled as if he had been carved out of stone. He didn't look at me now, just as he ignored me on the car ride home. "Why do you keep sleeping in here?" He turned to the bed and set his phone on the nightstand. "You can sleep down the hall."

I was in his t-shirt and my panties. "I don't want to sleep down the hall."

His green eyes looked foreboding when they looked at me like that. Intense and angry, they were passionate with frustration. He tugged the blankets back and got into bed beside me. A fire burned quietly in the fireplace and brought a gentle glow to the room once Cane turned off the lamp.

He turned on his side and faced away from me.

I missed the way he used to wrap his body around mine. I missed the suffocation he used to bring to me. I missed his affection, his adoration. I inched to the center of the bed and wrapped my arms around his waist. I pressed a wet kiss to his shoulder, my tongue tasting him. I tugged myself into him harder so my body was pressed flat against his.

His breathing increased, but he didn't show any other reaction.

I kissed his shoulder again then pressed my lips to his neck. I wanted to feel connected to him again. I missed having him close to me, missed sharing my body as well as my soul. But I also missed being with him. It'd only been a few weeks since Tristan last touched me, but my body craved Cane's. I wanted him deep inside me, slow and gentle. I wanted him to ease me into it, but then to bring me to a climax a few minutes later.

I moved my lips to his ear. "Make love to me."

Cane's body stiffened slightly, and he stopped breathing for just an instant. My hand rested just underneath his heart, and I could feel the way it jumped, racing at a faster pace. He didn't make a move, but he was certainly thinking about it.

"I'm ready."

He suddenly turned over and suspended his body over mine. He looked into my eyes, his powerful body flexing as he displayed his strength.

My hands moved up his chest, and I parted my lips, waiting for a kiss.

He tugged my panties down then separated my thighs with his. He positioned himself at my entrance but didn't push inside. Instead, he looked into my face and watched the expression in my eyes. "You're sure you want this?"

My hands dug into his hair, and I kissed him. It was slow and soft, and I felt his gentle mouth in contrast to the coarse stubble on his face. We breathed into each other before tongues were introduced. I shifted my hips slightly, grinding against his length. "Yes."

That was enough for him. He gripped one of my hips and tilted my body slightly so he could slip inside.

I was wet for him. I could feel him slide through my prominent slickness. If he wasn't sure how much I wanted this, he was certain now. My thoughts were only on the man above me, not on anyone who had been there before him.

He felt so good.

I'd missed this.

He moaned into my mouth as he inserted his entire

length. His lips stopped moving against mine as he held himself still, just enjoying me.

My hands slid down his powerful back, and I clawed his skin viciously.

He kissed the corner of my mouth then moved his kisses until he reached my ear. "I'll be gentle."

I rocked with him, taking in his length and moaning under my breath. "Just like that…"

He pinned his arms behind my knees and moved slowly, giving me all of his length before he pulled out again. He didn't pound me into the mattress the way he used to. He was gentler than he'd ever been before.

But it still felt incredible.

Cane suspended himself on one arm while his other hand dug into my hair. He held me possessively the way he used to and looked into my eyes as he thrust into me.

I never took my eyes away, watching his powerful physique shift and ripple with every movement. My hands moved to his chest, and I felt his heavy heartbeat, felt the passion inside his veins.

As if nothing had come between us to begin with, it felt like nothing was different. It was good. It was deep. It made my legs shake. It made my throat raspy from the insistent moans I made. He was thick and long, stretching me to my fullest. I might tear from a previous injury, but he felt so good I probably wouldn't notice.

"Cane…" My lips trembled, and I closed my eyes as the pleasure washed over me. I hadn't felt it in so long I almost didn't recognize it. It was more powerful than ever before, my body catching up on the goodness, when it only experienced the bad lately.

He didn't quicken his pace like he usually would, but the arousal was as obvious on his face as a billboard. His jaw was tight and rugged, and his eyes were narrowed and impassioned.

I kept going, my body writhing on the sheets where we used to make love all the time. My head rolled back, and I exposed my neck to his kisses, feeling his tongue delve into the hollow of my throat.

He kissed me until my climax had completely passed. Then he buried his face into my neck as he made his final thrusts. A moan erupted in his throat as he released inside me, giving me his mounds of desire. His teeth pressed against my neck as he devoured me with overwhelming urgency. His hand fisted my hair further, and he nearly yanked on it. He was possessive, territorial, and obsessed once again.

I'd missed that side of him.

It felt like us again, the two of us together.

He felt perfect buried between my legs. He felt like he belonged there, like he was the only one ever to have enjoyed me.

He turned his face into mine and kissed me softly on the lips, his affection gentle in comparison to the tight way he gripped me. He kissed the corner of my mouth then right on my lips again, covering me with his caresses.

He pulled out of me then cuddled into my side. His large arms encased me protectively, and he buried his face into my shoulder. There was no space between us because he was invading me completely.

It was exactly where I wanted to be, to be surrounded by his love and security.

Chapter 13

CANE

When I was buried deep inside her, it was impossible to stay angry at her.

I forgot I was mad to begin with.

That deep connection between us was exactly what I craved. It softened my thoughts, protected me from the gruesome things I'd seen during my adventure to rescue and guard her. It numbed the pain in my chest from seeing my brother bedridden.

It made everything easier.

I knew I wasn't treating Adelina fairly. I was hurt that she didn't feel the same way, but my anger existed because I felt deceived. I'd thought she really did feel the same way. Even now, I was surprised she didn't.

I felt tricked.

I was frustrated I wasn't getting my way.

But I shouldn't resent her for it. Even if she'd told me she didn't love me before she went to Tristan, I still would have risked my life to save her.

Because I had it bad.

I went to the gym in Florence the following morning and then swung by my other apartment. It'd been vacant for a while, possessing a stale air since it hadn't been used in so long. I grabbed a few things then headed back to my house in the Tuscan countryside.

When I walked in the door, Adelina was sitting at the kitchen table eating a piece of toast. Her eyes lit up when she saw me, looking over at me in my running shorts and t-shirt. I had a line of sweat around my neck from running six miles. "Hey."

"Hey." I walked over to her then leaned down and kissed her.

She softened visibly at my touch.

I opened the fridge and grabbed a carton of eggs. "I'm making an omelet. You want one?" I cracked the eggs into a bowl then got a pan going.

"No, thanks." She held her coffee between both hands, a small smile on her face. "I already ate."

"You ate a piece of toast," I said sarcastically. "That's not much."

"The coffee filled me up."

I made an egg white omelet with veggies then sat across from her with a hot cup of coffee.

"Where did you go this morning?"

"To the gym in Florence." I spoke between bites. "Then I stopped by my apartment and picked up a few things."

"You still have that place?"

"Yeah. I bought it a few years ago. Haven't decided what to do with it."

"So you like being away from the city?"

I liked having my privacy when I shared my space with this woman. I liked seeing her walk around in just her panties since there was no one to spy on us through the windows. I liked seeing her topless by the pool on a summer day. None of that could happen in the city. "It's nice. I understand why my brother prefers it."

"You own a lot of land. Are you going to grow grapes like your brother?"

"Probably. May as well use the space. Besides, it's got great landscaping."

"True."

"I think I've selected a butler for the house."

"Yeah?" She set her coffee down, visibly excited. "Who?"

"There's this older guy from Florence. He works in a high-end restaurant, but he says he wants something quieter. Both of his kids moved to France, and his ex-wife is remarried. So he says he's a bit lonely but doesn't want the crazy crowds anymore."

"He sounds perfect. Have you tried his cooking?"

"No, not yet. But he's been a chef his entire life. I'm not worried about his talents. He says it's important where he gets his products. Apparently, he's picky about those sorts of things, but they're important. I know Lars is the same way. He drives all the way to another town just to pick up his tomatoes, and then he goes to this other farm because of their asparagus…"

She smiled. "Wow. That's commitment."

"But the food is so good. Have you eaten over there?"

"No, I can't say I have."

"I'll rudely invite us over for lunch when Crow is feeling better."

She chuckled. "That's the nice thing about family. You don't need manners."

"Exactly." I leaned back against the wood of the chair and looked at her as I ate. I lived for the moments when she smiled like that. Her feelings for me in those instances didn't seem important. Maybe she didn't love me, but she was obviously fond of me. I had to have a special place in her heart after everything we'd been through together.

I finished my plate and placed it in the sink. "He'll be here later today. I'm gonna hop in the shower."

"Can I join you? You know…to save water."

I grinned at her then nodded toward the stairway. "Water conservation has always been a turn-on for me."

———

GERALD WAS a good fit the moment he stepped through the door. He was polite and right to the point, but he didn't overstep his boundaries by talking too much. He'd live in the downstairs bedroom with a private bathroom and living room, but he wouldn't make himself at home in the rest of the house.

He stuck to doing his job.

The place was spotless from the moment he arrived, and the first meal he made was tremendous. Succulent lamb chops and rice pilaf I hadn't had since my last visit to Greece. He kept the place immaculately clean, and as a result, it even smelled a little different.

It smelled better.

Now I wished I'd hired someone a long time ago. I wasn't a criminal anymore, so I had nothing to hide.

Gerald served dinner in the dining room, and the large window overlooked the front of the house and vineyards that stretched far into the distance. The closest house was a few miles away. The lights from their windows could be seen, but only subtly. Unless you already knew they were there, it would be difficult to make out.

Adelina sat across from me in a black dress with her straight hair curled at the ends. She did her makeup every day and seemed at ease in the house. She wasn't shaken and disturbed like she had been when she first returned to me. She made herself right at home.

"What do you think?"

She cut into the boneless rib and took a bite. "I don't want to insult you, but...he makes your cooking seem terrible."

I chuckled. "He makes your cooking look terrible too."

She smiled. "No offense taken. The only thing I'd make in my dorm was macaroni and Top Ramen."

"Top Ramen?"

"It's a soup thing."

Never heard of it.

"Gerald has a job guarantee for life," she said before she took another bite. "But he might make you fat."

If I didn't get started in the wine business soon, that might actually happen. I was running out of things to do. I could hit the gym and fuck Adelina all day, but that still wouldn't be enough. It'd only been a few weeks, but I missed the old business. I wondered how Constantine was handling it almost every single day.

She noticed the way my eyes shifted away. "What are you thinking about?"

"Work."

"Wine?"

"No. The other business." I sipped my glass of wine and tried to understand the boldness as well as the subtle sweetness. "I wonder how it's going. I haven't spoken to Bran about it."

"So you just forgot about it and moved on?"

"Pretty much."

"Why do you miss it so much?" she asked. "Was it the job, or was it because it was yours?"

I stared at my glass as I considered a response. "My dad started the business in his early twenties. He expected Crow

136

and me to take over. Vanessa was expected to stay home and have kids. We worked with him all the time until we grew into men. Then he and my mother were killed, but we never changed anything. So, it made me feel connected to him...in a way."

Her hand moved over mine. "I'm sorry."

"It was a long time ago. I won't pretend that my father was the best guy in the world, not the way other people always say. He wasn't faithful to my mother. He had slaves sometimes and hurt them. He cared about money, and he used his power for evil as well as for good."

She kept her hand on mine, her eyes trained on my face.

"I followed in his footsteps much more than Crow did. My dad and Crow fought a lot, which was why he opened the winery. Wanted to go his own way. I shared the same darkness my father did. I didn't have morals or rules. I fucked whores and slaves. I never considered my actions wrong because that was how I was raised. But now...I don't feel that way anymore." I pulled my hand away and turned back to my meal, not wanting to make Adelina upset. My transition started with Pearl and solidified when I laid eyes on Adelina.

Adelina continued to stare at me until she pulled her hand back to her side of the table.

I finished my food and looked out the window, suddenly feeling awkward. There was always tension in the room due to the silent understanding we had with one another. It was difficult to ignore when we were both thinking about it—all the time.

"Did you have a good childhood?"

"Yeah," she said immediately. "I was an only child, so all I ever had was my parents' attention and affection. My mama was a stay-at-home mom, so she was always around. We'd make cookies on Sundays, she'd help me with my homework during the week because she's much brighter than people realize, and she'd drive me and my friends around on Saturdays. My dad is more on the quiet side, but he's very funny. I don't have a single bad thing to say about either one of them."

Our lives couldn't be much more different. "That sounds nice."

"My parents did a great job. I always imagined being like my mom when I have kids..." The tension filled the space again because we both knew she imagined having kids with someone other than me.

I brushed it off. "You want to help me out at the winery?"

"Tomorrow?" she asked.

"I mean in general. Crow said we should expand the business by buying more land and setting up a second winery. It's something we can do together. You've been helping out over there, so I'm sure you know a thing or two."

She flicked her food around with her fork. "When were you planning on doing this?"

"Probably over the next few months. I have to wait for Crow to be well again, and then we'll purchase the property…and go from there."

She stared at her food and set her fork down. Her plate wasn't empty, and she usually ate everything before she was done. Her shoulders were hunched, and her head was downcast. Her fingers rubbed against her neck, and that smile she wore minutes ago was long gone.

"Everything okay?"

"Yeah… I just…" She ran her fingers through her hair nervously, avoiding eye contact with me.

She wasn't the kind of woman to drop her gaze, no matter what kind of foe she faced. "What?"

"I assumed I would be going back home…" She pulled her hand from her soft strands and finally looked me in the eye.

The thought hadn't crossed my mind—not once. I just assumed she would stay with me, after everything we'd been through. I'd saved her from Tristan, and I thought we'd live the rest of our lives together. She didn't love me, but she would live a comfortable life with my wealth and protection.

She continued to watch me, tense as if I might explode.

"Go back home? To tell Lizzie's parents what happened?" I suppose she deserved to tell her parents that she was okay, that she was being treated well and had the freedom to do what she wanted. She wasn't the property of a psychopath anymore.

"Yeah...and because that's where I live."

She wanted to leave me. After everything I'd done for her, she wanted to go back to her old life.

"I could go back to school and be a teacher. I could spend time with my parents again. I could have my life back...the life I had before everything was taken away from me."

All I could do was stare at her in surprise. I wasn't sure why the thought had never crossed my mind. Why would I expect her to stay here with me if she wasn't in love with me?

"I thought I could stay a little longer, maybe a week or so. But I should be getting back."

Those words hurt most of all. It was hard enough being with a woman who didn't share my feelings, but watching her walk away after what I did for her was a punch in the gut. "Do you understand what I did for you?" I spoke quietly, but the words were pregnant with audible rage. My hands trembled on the table, and every muscle in my back was tense and rigid.

"Yes, and I—"

"While you were sitting here eating everything in my fridge, I was killing every man I locked eyes with to get my brother out of there. My brother was tortured and beaten because he risked his neck for you. He risked his wife for you. No, Adelina. I don't think you grasp the severity of the situation." I rose out of my chair even though I had no idea why I did. My body couldn't sit still anymore. There was so much anger pumping through my veins. "I lost my business because of you."

Her eyes filled with moisture until she couldn't look at me anymore.

"After all of that, you just leave?"

Her mouth was shut tight, her body trembling slightly.

"When I walked into that room where you were hand-cuffed to the wall, I could have fucked you. I didn't. When I took you as a loan, I could have done whatever I wanted to you. Did I? No. When you were in my captivity, you were shown nothing but respect. I took you sight-seeing and made your life enjoyable. And when I turned you over to Tristan, I was sick to my stomach. I couldn't sleep knowing you were there. So I risked everything to get you back. I risked my whole family—for you."

It was the first time she'd cowered underneath me, appearing small and fragile.

My hands were shaking because I was so angry. She'd played me for a fool, used me for everything that I had. I was tougher than stone and never let my guard down for anyone. The first time I did, she stabbed me right in the gut. She used me, played me. I was just a stepping-stone to get where she wanted. I wasn't going to sacrifice so much unless I got something out of it. "You aren't going back, Adelina. You were Tristan's prisoner, and now you're mine. That's your debt to me."

She looked up at me again, and this time, her eyes flashed. "You can't be serious."

"I am serious." I'd never meant anything more in my life. "You're my property. I'm not the kind of man who does something for free. I always expect something in return. I saved your life, declared war against an ally, and lost my family's business to save you. You bet your ass, you're staying. If you ask me, you got a good deal."

"Cane, I have a family—"

"I don't give a shit. You'll have a beautiful house to live in, more money than you know what to do with, and you'll be at my beck and call. Much better than being in Tristan's captivity, if you ask me. I'm done being a nice guy, and I'll never be a nice guy again." I stormed away from the table and knocked over the glass of wine as I made my exit. I'd never felt so stupid in my life. If she didn't love me, I could accept that. But to return home to her life like nothing happened infuriated me. I'd put everything on the line for this woman, and she wanted to leave me behind and forget about it.

I almost lost everything because of her.

Because of my stupidity.

But never again.

Never again.

———

SHE MUST HAVE STAYED in her old bedroom because she never joined me in mine.

Good. I didn't want her there.

The next day, I was just as angry as I had been the night before. In fact, I was even angrier. I couldn't imagine the look on my brother's face if I told him Adelina was going home like nothing ever happened. Crow would know he'd risked his family for absolutely nothing.

Nothing.

I did everything I could to save Pearl, but that was because she was my sister-in-law. She was family.

Adelina was just some whore.

A whore who played me.

I put a transmitter inside of her when she first arrived here, but I never used it. She didn't try to run, and when she went back to Tristan, I already knew where she was. I went downstairs and she was nowhere in sight. I opened my laptop. I opened the program and found the tracker information.

It was still working.

Adelina didn't show her face for hours, so I went upstairs to make sure she didn't make a run for it. I opened her bedroom without knocking and found her sitting on the bed, wearing a t-shirt with a somber expression on her face.

"Come here."

She stared at me defiantly, her soft expression hardening into a glare. "No."

When she fought me, it both aroused me and irritated me. "Don't make me ask again, Adelina. You know I enjoy pulling on that beautiful hair of yours." I'd drag her all the way down the stairs if she made me. She'd blown a fuse in my brain, and now my wiring was destroyed. I wasn't the same person I was before. I was a whole new man.

She knew our situation was different now. When she first arrived here, she called my bluffs because she identified my true character. But she knew she couldn't call my bluff this time.

She got out of bed and slowly walked to the doorway.

I didn't wait for her and took the stairs to the main living room. I turned the laptop toward her and pointed to the map on the screen. "This is you. I can see where you are at all times. Run, and see what happens." I shut the laptop. "I've swept the house for weapons. You won't find any guns anywhere, and if you manage to get your hands on one, you better get in at least six shots. I've been shot before. Didn't do much." Even if there were a gun around, I knew she wouldn't shoot me. She was pissed at me, but I'd risked everything to save her. She wouldn't cross me like that.

"I know you're mad right now, but you need to calm down and come to your senses."

I crossed my arms over my chest and stared down at her. "I'm calm, Adelina. You'll know when I'm not."

"The Cane I know wouldn't do this."

"The Cane you knew is dead. You played him for a fool, and now he's gone."

"I didn't play him." Her beautiful brown eyes brightened when she spoke emotionally. She was either being honest or was desperate to be free. "I care about him. Just because I want to go home doesn't mean I don't want to be with you. It doesn't mean I don't have feelings for you."

"I don't care about any of that. You should get comfortable. I'm not changing my mind."

"What about my parents?"

"What about them?" I countered. "I let you see them one last time."

She shook her head, giving me a fierce look of disappointment. "You're better than this."

"No, I'm not. And I couldn't care less about your opinion—not anymore."

She stepped closer to me, straightening her spine so she seemed a little taller. "I never asked you to save me, Cane. I never asked you to accept me as part of a loan. When you dropped me off at Tristan's, I never expected you to come back for me. You did all those things on your own. You shouldn't have expected anything."

"Well, I do expect something. Is being with me that horrible, Adelina?"

Her eyes narrowed before they softened.

"You'd rather be with him? Is that what you're telling me? You wish you were still lying on that cot with your ankle locked to the wall?" I remembered the night I broke her out of there. I found her helpless and weak. She was treated like a dog much more than a human.

"No. But I want Cane back...my Cane. I want the man who's better than all those assholes. I want the man who's always respected me and taken care of me. I want the man who has a huge heart that he's always trying to hide. I want him back…"

"He's gone. I already told you that."

"I'm sorry that you risked everything——"

"No, you aren't. All you care about is yourself."

Her eyes snapped wide again. "If I only cared about myself, I would have run away a long time ago. I stayed to help my friend Lizzie. How dare you call me selfish when I was raped every single day just for the slim possibility that it could save her. I'm much braver than you'll ever be, Cane." She flashed me a hostile look of disappointment before she stepped back. "When I tell Pearl and Crow, they won't let you do this."

I shook my head. "They won't interfere."

"You bet your ass, they will."

"When you last saw Crow, do you remember what you said to him?"

Her expression shifted at my words. She stared at me with suspicion, like she didn't know why there'd been a sudden change.

"You told him you were in debt to him for what he did for you. Why didn't you say the same to me?"

Her eyes fell.

I repeated the question. "Why didn't you say the same to me, Adelina?" I stepped closer to her, my shadow covering her. "Why does he get your debt, but I don't? I was the one who begged him to help me. I was the one who lost ten million dollars. I was the one who handed over my business to protect you." I pressed my face closer to hers. "Answer me."

"I am grateful for what you did, Cane. I never said I wasn't."

"Tell me you're indebted to me," I whispered. "If there's anything I ever need, you'll make it happen."

She stared at me silently.

"Say it."

"Thank you for saving me, Cane. If there's anything I can do, let me know…"

"Thank you for the offer," I said coldly. "There is something you can do for me. You're going to be mine—for the rest of your life."

———

CROW SAT on the couch across from me in his study and set the decanter of scotch on the table. He still wasn't drinking, but he wouldn't deny me the pleasure. The flames burned in the fireplace even though it was midafternoon. Crow was still weak, but at least he could get around the house now.

I made myself a drink and let it slide down my throat.

Crow watched me with a dark expression.

"I'm not trying to rub it in, I promise."

Crow leaned back and rubbed his fingers against his temple. "I can't remember the last time I had a drink. My liver is confused."

"Good. Maybe you'll live a little longer."

"I don't know. I should have died a long time ago."

I chuckled. "We both should have."

When Crow shifted his position on the couch, he stiffened in pain for a moment. His jaw tightened, and a look of displeasure spread across his face.

"How are you coming along?"

"It's alright," he said quietly. "Just bored."

"I thought we could start on the new site for the vineyard."

"Pearl wouldn't go for that."

I opened the folder I brought with me and set it in front of him. "I mapped out the best locations based on soil quality, tourism, etc. Some of the prime spots are more expensive, but I think they'll be worth it. The last one is the best choice. It's only twenty miles east of here."

Crow looked over my selection silently. He flipped through each page, his face a wall of stoicism. "I'm surprised you did all this research. With Adelina around, I didn't think you'd have the time."

"I can only fuck that woman so many times."

Crow's eyes flicked up to mine at my choice of words. I didn't talk about Adelina that way to anyone, just as he didn't talk about Pearl. But now, she didn't mean anything to me. I didn't respect her, not when she'd cut me so deeply. "Everything alright?"

"Yeah." I took another drink. "What do you think about the last one?"

His eyes returned to the folder. "It's a good choice. I think we should do it."

"I can put the bid in and make the arrangements."

"I need to see it first."

"Then let's go."

"I can't," he said with a sigh. "Until these stitches come out, I'm not moving."

"Since when did Pearl start running the show?"

He shrugged. "Since the day I met her, probably."

I chuckled. "At least you admit it."

"How are things going with Adelina? Is she adjusting...?"

"She's fine." I took another drink, covering up the annoyance I felt toward her.

Crow saw the anger in my eyes when no one else picked up on it. "Why do you get so tense every time she's mentioned?"

"Maybe because I don't want to talk about her."

Crow rubbed his jaw as he studied my features. "What happened, Cane?"

"Nothing. I'll talk to Pearl about letting you see that property with me."

"You don't need to ask her permission. That's not the problem."

"Then what is the problem?"

"I agree that I shouldn't go anywhere. Until I'm in the clear, I shouldn't be exposed to unnecessary bacteria. I haven't gotten an infection, and I want to keep it that way."

I wanted my brother to get better, but I wanted to move forward. "How much more time do you need?"

"My next checkup is in a week. That's when the stitches will be removed."

"We'll stop by then."

"Sounds good to me," he said. "Now that we've established that, let's circle back to Adelina. And don't change the subject this time."

I gripped my glass as I held it on my thigh. "There's nothing to say."

"I can tell you're pissed, and I want to know why. Now, tell me."

"I'm not pissed." I downed the entire contents and set the glass on the coffee table. "I should get going. I'll check in later this week to see how you're doing."

Crow stared at me coldly. "I'm just going to find out some other way."

"I'm sure you will."

———

I HIT the gym then returned home. Gerald had lunch prepared for me, so I scarfed it down before I went upstairs. Adelina didn't hang out outside her room. She stayed in there nearly all the time, adamantly avoiding me.

I stopped by her room and opened the door.

She was sitting in an armchair by the fire, reading. She looked up when I entered, her guard up. "Can I help you?"

"You're free to move through the rest of the house. Gerald told me you stay in here all day."

She turned her gaze back to her book. "I like it in here."

"I'll be back after I take a shower. I expect you to be stripped down to your panties on the bed, ass up and face down."

She stared at me with an expression as cold as ice, but deep inside, I saw a glimmer of a flame. She hated me right now, but her body could never hate the things I did to her.

"This is the part where you say, 'Yes, sir.'"

She continued to glare.

I left the doorway and walked toward her, my need for dominance making me want to grip her by the neck. I stopped in front of her, my hands by my sides. "Yes, sir."

"No."

I grabbed her neck and forced her to look up at me. "Fight me, and see what happens." I squeezed her gently, applying enough pressure so she knew I wasn't issuing idle threats. This woman betrayed me, and now I despised her. She ruined me. She made me believe in good until she gave me a reason not to believe in anything anymore.

She took a deep breath and turned her head away from me, trying to get free of my hold. "Yes, sir."

My hand moved to the back of her neck, and I yanked her back. "Good girl." I kissed her on the mouth before I walked away, feeling my fingers ache from where I had gripped her. I wanted to smack her ass with these fingers, to grip her while I took her then and there.

But it would have to wait until I was done in the shower.

———

WHEN I ENTERED HER ROOM, she was in just her panties like I asked. She was on all fours on the bed, her feet hanging over the edge.

I stared at her luscious ass before I shut the door and stripped off my clothes. My heart had turned off, and now all I saw was a gorgeous woman about to take my cock. She was just like all the others who meant nothing to me.

I came up behind her and leaned over her body, pressing kisses up her spine to the back of her neck. My hand groped her tit, and I felt her lack of reaction. She was perfectly still, fighting me with quiet resistance.

That wouldn't last long.

She'd enjoyed fucking me just a few days ago, initiating every single round. As pissed as she was, I knew she wanted me.

She would always want me.

I pushed the head of my cock inside her and felt the wetness greet me. She was warm, tight, and so damn wet.

She wanted me.

I moved inside her until I was completely sheathed. My hand slid around her neck, and I jerked her head up so she was looking at the ceiling. My lips found her ear, and I breathed into her canal. "You want me."

She breathed hard as I held her in place.

"Tell me you want me."

Silence.

I gripped her throat a little tighter, forcing her to give in.

"I want you…"

I didn't need to hear her say it because her body betrayed her. She was gushing at her opening, her cream sheathing me to the hilt. I started to thrust into her, to give her deep and even strokes. I explored her body with my length, hitting her over and over again. In record-breaking time, I would make her come—like always.

This was easier. I wasn't sure what I had been thinking, falling for a woman. Relationships were only a weakness. She cost me one of the most important things in my life— my family's legacy. I wouldn't make the same mistake twice. Now she was just a slave, a woman I would keep until I became bored of her.

If I ever grew bored of her.

Chapter 14

PEARL

Crow stood at the bathroom sink with a towel wrapped around his waist. He looked at himself in the mirror and shaved his face, removing the thick stubble that had developed over the past week. His green eyes watched his movements, and he slowly sliced away the line of hair before he rinsed off his razor in the sink.

His muscular physique remained the same even though he'd been in bed for a while. His stomach was still sculpted despite the stitches along his abdomen. The cast had been removed, but he still couldn't make sudden movements. The only part of his body that seemed to have completely healed was his leg. He could stand on it without losing his balance anymore.

I was in the bathroom picking up dirty towels, but I got distracted looking at him.

His eyes flicked to mine in the reflection. "Yes, Button?"

"I can't stare at you?" I asked, cocking my head to the side. "I am married to you."

"I'm the only one that does the staring. That's how this works."

"I don't remember agreeing to that."

"I agreed for you." He set his razor aside and splashed water onto his face, removing the shaving cream so he could pat his face down with a towel. He yanked the towel from around his waist and dropped it in my arms, where a bundle of towels already sat. Beautiful and buck naked, he walked past me, wearing a cocky grin on his face.

I turned around and watched him go, seeing his hard ass as he walked away.

I'd never get tired of looking at that. "How's your pain?"

"Five."

"That's a big improvement."

He pulled on a pair of boxers. "Yeah. It was the first time I slept through the night last night."

I hated knowing he was in pain, but I knew it would pass eventually. We just needed to get through a few more weeks, and he would be back to normal. "That's good."

"Cane wants me to go look at a property with him."

"A property for what?"

He opened his closet and pulled on a t-shirt. "For the winery. We're opening a second location."

"I didn't know that."

"I guess I forgot to mention it."

"So you'll be in business together again?"

He grabbed a pair of black jeans and pulled them on. "Yeah. Since he lost the business, I think it's the best thing for both of us. I could use the help, and he needs a purpose. Losing the weapons business was devastating because it belonged to our father. With the winery, it'll be a family business again."

"That's true. I think it's a good idea."

"But we'll also have our own space so we don't kill each other." He grabbed his wallet and keys and placed them in his pocket.

I looked him up and down. "It looks like you're going somewhere...and you know you aren't going anywhere."

Crow wore a hard smile that made him look more handsome than usual. "Button, the doctor said I was fine."

"No harm in taking it easy."

"I can't sit around anymore. I hate watching TV, and I'm not a big fan of books."

"Because you can't read?" I teased.

His eyes narrowed but in a playful way. "You're asking for it, Button."

"Am I?" Our sex life hadn't been great lately. Anytime he made a move, I pushed off his advance because I didn't want to risk him injuring himself. But I was definitely going crazy. I was only a month pregnant and the hormones hadn't kicked in yet, but I definitely had a distinct craving for him.

"Yes, you are." He walked up to me and gripped both of my ass cheeks with his large hands. "And I'm more than happy to give it to you."

I tossed the bundle of towels on the bed and wrapped my arms around his neck. I kissed him softly, making sure the kiss didn't escalate into something I couldn't walk away from. When Crow had something on his mind, it was impossible to get him to stop. "Maybe later. I know you should get going." I moved away from his embrace and licked my lips.

He stared me down with an intense expression, wanting something he couldn't have. "I'm not going to keep waiting, Button."

"You're supposed to take it easy."

"Like I give a damn. I want to fuck my wife."

"That's romantic."

He grabbed my chin and directed my gaze to his. "You know we make it romantic." His eyes shifted back and forth between mine before he pressed another kiss to my lips. It was quick and subtle but enough to make my blood warm. "When I get back, you're getting on my lap, and you're gonna fuck me hard. Do you understand?"

He was so bossy, but I liked him that way. "Yes, husband. I understand."

———

LARS KNOCKED on the open bedroom door and didn't step inside. "Mrs. Barsetti, Miss Adelina is here to see you."

"She is?" I'd just finished placing the laundry in all the drawers and organizing the towels in the bathroom. Cane already picked up Crow, so she must have brought her own car over here. "I'll be down in a second."

I headed to the entryway on the first floor and found her standing there in jeans and a t-shirt. Instead of wearing that beaming smile I'd come to know her for, she had her arms crossed over her chest, and she looked over her shoulder like someone would sneak up on her any minute. "Hey."

When she realized I was there, she turned to me and gave me a warmer greeting. "Hey, Pearl."

"What's up? Wanted to hang out while the men are away?"

"Something like that." She put on a smile, but I could tell it was forced.

"Have you eaten? I was just about to sit down."

"Yeah, that would be nice. Cane always says Lars is quite the cook."

"Great." I guided her into the dining room, and we took a seat. Instantly, Lars brought fresh bread, butter, a bottle of wine, and two glasses of water. He exited the room again, attending to the entrees that would be done any minute.

I took a piece of bread, and so did she. I couldn't have the wine, but she helped herself to it.

"How's Crow doing?"

"He's restless and frustrated, but he's good. Give it a little more time, and he'll be back to his old self."

"That's good to hear. I know he's been through a lot, and I'm glad he's recovered so quickly."

"I'm excited for it to be over. He'll be happy to jog in the morning and get back to work. He's not the kind of guy that likes to sit around and do nothing."

"I noticed," she said with a chuckle. "How's the baby?"

"Everything feels the same," I said honestly. "I get sick in the morning sometimes, but other than that, I don't really feel pregnant yet."

"Maybe you should go in for a checkup."

"I will. I just wanted to wait until Crow was feeling better. I don't want to bring him to a doctor's office until he's completely healed. And he wouldn't want to miss it."

"You're right." She kept tearing the bread into pieces without taking a single bite.

I noticed her fidgety movements and recognized that wasn't normal for her. She was usually controlled and confident, engaging in conversation while holding my gaze. "Everything alright, Adelina? I get the impression something is wrong."

"Something is wrong," she said bluntly. "It's Cane."

I knew he was upset that she hadn't said what he wanted to hear, but he would get over it eventually. "Yeah?"

"I told him I wanted to go back home. I have family there, and I want to go back to school…"

She didn't need to finish for me to figure out exactly what happened. I hadn't thought about her leaving. For some reason, I imagined she would stay in Tuscany with the three of us just the way I stayed with Crow. But she had a life to get back to. I didn't have anyone. Our situations were completely different. She was a few years younger than me, too.

"He got really upset," she whispered. "I mean, he completely changed into a different person. He said it was wrong that he'd done so much for me, and I was just going to walk away. He said he lost his business because of me. He said he almost lost his brother because of me."

"He's just upset. It'll blow over."

She shook her head. "He said he's not going to ever let me go. He said I'm his prisoner now...that I'm indebted to him."

It was hard for me to believe that because it didn't seem like something Cane would say. When I first met him, I wouldn't have put it past him to act that way. He hadn't had compassion the way he did now. But to say something like that after everything we'd been through didn't sound right. "I can't believe that..."

She nodded. "I thought it would blow over in a few days, but he's not letting up. He has a tracker in my arm, and he threatened me not to try to run. I sleep in my own room down the hall, and he doesn't speak to me much. He just demands sex when he wants it...then goes about his daily life. We aren't close like we used to be. He's completely pushed me away, shut me out. I don't feel the connection we used to have. We used to talk...to tell each other things. We used to make love. But now, all of that is over...he's not the same. He snapped and turned into a completely different person."

The piece of bread was still between my fingers, but I didn't take a bite. I wasn't even hungry anymore. Lars stepped into the room and placed our entrees in front of us, but neither one of us acknowledged him. It was quiet until he left the room again. "But he knows Crow and I would never let that happen."

"I told him that, but he didn't care. He said there's nothing you guys can do about it."

I couldn't go to the police or threaten him to release her. But I could certainly talk to him. "I'm surprised this happened."

"I know. He's not the Cane I met. When I first met him, I knew he was better than all the others. I knew he had a soft spot, a soul. He was always so good to me, so thoughtful. And to see him like this... It's scary."

"Cane used to be a bad man. But those days are over."

"They were over," she said. "But now they're back. I set him off, and now he's a different person. I really don't think he's ever going to let me go."

I ignored the ravioli placed in front of us and felt the steam waft up and hit my face. I knew Cane was hurt when Adelina said she didn't love him, but I didn't know it would push him this far. "I'll talk to him."

"Please. I tried to explain to him that I care about him. My wanting to leave has nothing to do with him. If my parents lived down the street, I'd stay with him. But they live on a completely different continent. I can't stay here just for him, even if I do have feelings for him. That's all. I think he thinks he doesn't mean anything to me...which just isn't true."

"Maybe he doesn't understand that," I said quietly. "I'll talk to him. I'll get this whole thing sorted out."

"Thank you. When I try to talk to him, he doesn't listen to me."

Cane had really gone off the deep end to act this way. It took him so long to shift from being a ruthless criminal to a compassionate hero. It would be a shame to wipe all of that away for nothing.

"Do you think he's right?" she whispered.

"What?"

"He did so much for me...and I owe him."

"No, Adelina. You don't owe him anything. He did those things for you because he cared about you. You never asked him to save you. I know he would have done it anyway even if he knew your relationship was going to end."

"I'm not so sure," she whispered. "You'll see what I mean when you talk to him."

"Okay."

"Crow might be able to help, too, but I feel bad for asking since he's been through so much."

"He doesn't mind. Crow is the one person in the world Cane will listen to. We can use that to our advantage."

She reached across the table and placed her hand on mine. "Thanks so much for helping me. I feel bad for asking since you guys have already done so much."

"Don't feel bad. We don't mind at all. Really."

She pulled her hand away and looked down at her food. She reached for her fork and finally took a bite. "It's pretty good."

"Lars made me put on ten pounds after I moved in."

She chewed another bite. "But it was totally worth it. This is delicious." She poked at the food in the bowl then looked up at me again. "Sometimes I think I could love him. But after this happened...it made me realize it's better that I don't."

My heart fell into my stomach when I heard what she said. If Cane had just been patient like I told him, things could have been different. But he let his anger get to him, and now he'd pushed her away. I couldn't blame her for feeling this way.

Who could?

———

WHEN CANE PULLED up to the front of the house in his black car, I walked outside and met them at the round-about. As if Crow wasn't still severely injured, he got out of the car and held himself perfectly upright, like there was nothing holding him back at all.

He looked at me with slight amusement in his eyes, as though he thought my concern was comical. "Button."

I stood on my tiptoes and gave him a quick kiss. The embrace would have lasted longer if I weren't upset. Adelina had already left and drove back to Cane's house, so I could speak to him without her there.

Crow pulled away and knew something was wrong. "What is it?"

Cane walked around the car, in a leather jacket with sunglasses sitting on the bridge of his nose. I didn't notice it before, but he did seem distinctly different. His shoulders were more rigid, he wore a grimace rather than a smile, and he seemed moody—just the way Crow was. He came to our side and stood beside Crow. "We took a look at the property and liked what we saw. Our earth science guy said the soil composition was perfect."

"That's great." I couldn't care less about the property they were acquiring, at least, not right now. "So, Adelina stopped by..."

Cane's expression didn't change, but I couldn't see his eyes behind his glasses.

I crossed my arms over my chest. "Had some very interesting things to say."

Cane stared at me in silence.

Crow turned to his brother, obviously having no idea what was going on.

"I'm gonna give you the benefit of the doubt to explain your behavior," I said. "And to tell me you're just angry and this will blow over once you come to your senses."

"I'm not going to come to my senses," he said simply. "I risked everything to save that woman, and in return, I get to keep her. That's her payment for my sacrifice. I'm not the kind of guy who hands out charity. I didn't do all of that so she could go back to her life in America and forget about me." His attitude shifted and was noticeably dark. He obviously didn't care about my opinion on the matter. Adelina was right when she said he'd flipped a switch. It seemed like I was talking to Cane from two years ago, the ruthless barbarian who didn't hesitate to beat me to within an inch of my life.

Crow eyed his brother, his eyebrow raised.

"That's wrong, and you know it."

"I know it's wrong." He shrugged. "But I don't give a damn."

I shifted my gaze to Crow, silently asking him for help.

Crow picked up on my request and turned to his brother. "So, what's your plan? To keep her locked up in your house all day?"

"Yep."

"And you don't think she'll run?" Crow asked.

"I put a tracker in her," Cane said simply. "And she knows what I'll do if she tries to run." The threat was so easy, rolling off his tongue like it meant nothing.

"I thought the reason why we saved her was because you loved her," Crow said.

"I did, at one point." Cane looked at the house, shifting his gaze elsewhere. "Not anymore."

"You don't just stop loving someone," I snapped. "When you love someone the way you love her, you can't stop. It's always there, no matter how much you try to fight it. Keeping her like a dog isn't right. You don't do that to someone you love."

"Which is why I don't love her," Cane countered. "She's just a woman I fuck. That's it. That's her only job. If she embraces the situation, she can get a lot out of it. She can be a wealthy woman living in Tuscany. I can take her to see the world, give her a lifestyle she could never afford on a teacher's salary."

"Money isn't everything." I didn't love Crow because of his wealth. I loved him because I was as broken as he was. He fixed me, put me back together so I was more whole than I had been before I was broken. "I can tell it doesn't mean anything to Adelina."

"That's a shame," Cane said. "She might be bored, then. Not my problem."

I wanted to slap him upside the head. "Knock it off, Cane. You're being a dickhead."

"Because I am a dickhead," he said simply. "Pussy Cane is over. The real one is back."

"No one likes the old Cane," I snarled. "He's an asshole who doesn't care about anyone but himself. You've grown so much over the past year. You're really going to throw that all away just because you didn't get what you wanted? Did it ever occur to you that maybe Adelina is just scared to love you? That she needs to come to the realization on her own?"

Cane's cold ferocity disappeared. He turned his face back to me, looking me in the eye through his shades. "What the hell is that supposed to mean?"

"She wants to go back because she wants to see her family. She wants them to know she's okay. She wants to be there for Lizzie's parents. But when she gets there, she'll realize it's not home anymore. After everything she's been through, she knows she doesn't belong there anymore. The only person who truly understands her is you. That's when she'll come back. But you have to be patient, and turning into a controlling psychopath is only going to sabotage your chance to really be with her. So, cut the bullshit. I'm not buying this act."

Crow watched his brother, his hands in his pockets. "I let Pearl go once. She went to America, and I let her be. We both knew being apart wasn't right for either of us. We came back together because that's where we belonged. If you love this woman, you have to let her go."

"And don't say you don't love her because we both know you do," I barked. "You sacrificed everything for her, and in return, she made you into a better man. Don't piss that all away. Get your act together, and maybe Adelina will forgive you."

Cane stayed still with his arms crossed, as if these words meant nothing to him. Even though he wore a stoic expression, I was sure he was thinking behind those shades. Thoughts had to be swirling.

"Cane," I pressed. "There's still time to fix this. You're better than this."

"You are," Crow said. "Give her a chance to come back to you. That's how you'll know it's true."

"She doesn't love me," Cane finally said. "She won't come back."

"If that's what happens, that's what happens," I whispered. "But keeping her a prisoner against her will won't get you what you want. The sex won't be the same. The conversation won't be the same. She told me she misses the way you used to be, the way you used to feel connected."

His jaw clenched slightly, and he shifted his gaze to the ground.

"Whether she loves you or not, the woman does care about you. She does think of you as a hero. You mean something to her. Don't destroy her opinion of you by turning into the monster she just got away from."

Like I'd said something particularly offensive, he snapped. "I would never hit her. I'm not barbaric."

"And holding her against her will isn't barbaric?" Crow countered.

Cane turned his gaze on his brother, holding a long pause full of rage. "You're one to talk."

"I didn't love Pearl at the time," Crow argued. "So it's not the same."

"Go home and make this right, Cane," I said. "Before it's too late and you can't fix it."

He stepped back and sighed, his large hand moving through his hair. "Maybe you're right…"

I was relieved we got through to him. I knew Cane was better than this. Reverting back to the criminal man he used to be wasn't the answer. It might make him feel better because he didn't feel anything at all, but that wasn't going to solve his problem. Once the anger passed, he would just feel guilty for what he'd done to the one woman he cared about. And by then, he would be lost to her forever.

Cane turned away from us and walked back to the car, his shoulders hunched and his back not as rigid as before. He didn't say goodbye before he got into the car.

The two of us were left in the roundabout, watching the dirt fly up from Cane's tires. He hit the road and drove away, his powerful engine loud enough for us to hear him even when he was miles away.

When I looked at Crow, he was already looking at me. And it seemed like he'd been staring at me for a while.

"I don't blame him for reacting that way. He was frustrated and didn't know how to handle it."

"Don't justify his behavior."

"I'm not. I'm just saying I understand. Cane and I come from a background where we take what we want. The only successful relationship he's ever seen is the two of us. I kept you for so long that you eventually started to love me, for all the good and the bad. Maybe he thought if he kept her longer, she would change her mind."

"That would be wrong."

Crow gazed off into the distance, looking tall with his broad shoulders and muscular stature. He watched until his brother was a simple dot in the distance. He turned back to me. "I've known Cane my whole life. He struggles with emotions more than I do, not because he doesn't feel them, but because he feels them a million times stronger. I kept my composure when Vanessa died in my arms. I didn't shed a tear for my parents. I've never really felt anything until you. He cares more than he wants to admit, and because of that, he hurts a lot more. To love someone the way he loves her and to not feel that love back...is more than he can stand. I'm not excusing his behavior. I'm just explaining it. If one day you decided to walk out on me...I'm not sure what I would do. Probably lock you up too."

I smiled because he would never have to worry about that. "You can lock me up whenever you want."

He didn't give me a smile back, but he gave me a scorching expression instead. It was intense and dangerous, one of my favorite looks. "Be careful, Button."

"You know I'm never careful when it comes to you."

I DRIED my hair with a towel wrapped around my body.

Once my strands were completely dry, I stepped into the bedroom and searched my drawer for a pair of underwear. I found a lacy black thong, so I dropped my towel and pulled it on. Sometimes I thought my stomach looked different, and today, it seemed a little rounder than usual.

But that could just be my imagination.

A searing gaze penetrated my skin and burned the surface. I could feel the stare, just like a vulnerable animal separated from the herd felt the presence of a predator. My eyes turned to the doorway, and I saw Crow standing there, looking at me with a pair of eyes so dark they were terrifying.

I held his gaze, too timid to move.

He suddenly lurched at me, grabbed me by the arm, and threw me down on the bed. My panties were yanked off, and he dropped his jeans in an instant. His boxers were pulled down his ass, and he yanked me to the edge of the bed. "I'm not waiting anymore. I could give myself another hernia, and I wouldn't give a damn." He shoved himself inside me, gripped me by the back of the neck, and then fucked me like he hadn't had me in years rather than days.

Any time we were together lately, it was gentle and slow. I was always the one on top because I didn't want him to move too vigorously. All I cared about was him healing properly. But when he pinned me down and took me like this, I didn't want to fight.

I just wanted to be taken.

He anchored his muscular arms behind my knees and

leaned over me, hitting me deep and hard every time. The last thing he wanted to do was make love to me. He wanted to fuck me senseless, make me so sore I couldn't walk for the rest of the day. His eyes locked on me, and the muscles of his body shifted underneath his skin as he thrust. He dominated me like an unstoppable man, getting exactly what he wanted without waiting for an answer. He yanked on the back of my hair and forced my chin up so he could plaster my neck with kisses and soft bites. He smothered the hollow of my throat as he kept going, hitting me in the perfect spot repeatedly. His hand released my hair, and he moved to my stomach. He wasn't aggressive when he touched me, his fingers softly exploring the surface. I wasn't swollen like a pregnant woman in her second or third trimester, but I knew why Crow was touching me. He leaned down and pressed a kiss to my tummy before he straightened and started fucking me again, gripping my tits and securing my hair around his fingers again.

My hands explored the muscles under his shirt, but I didn't dig my nails into his skin. I lightly touched him as I felt his body rub against my clit. I looked into his eyes and watched him fuck me like an animal, and he took me to a place where all I could do was moan and scream. My pussy choked his cock as I squeezed him hard, bringing me to a climax that was so powerful I writhed. "Crow…"

He grabbed my neck and bored his gaze into mine. "Mrs. Barsetti."

My orgasm stretched on for a while, spiraling and

exploding. I felt so warm, hot and sweaty in a phenomenal way. My pussy was still tight around his cock, and I was floating on waves of pleasure. It was so good. "Come inside me." I grabbed his hips and yanked him hard into me over and over, wanting him to finish by filling me with all of his arousal.

He pounded into me as he brought himself to orgasm. A deep and masculine moan escaped his throat, and he shoved himself deep so he could give me all of his seed. He pressed his forehead to mine as he pushed me into the mattress, his cock twitching as he squirted.

My fingers dug into his hips, loving the heaviness he'd just given me.

He caught his breath before he pressed a quick kiss to my lips. He held himself over me and stared down at me, the possessiveness still in his eyes. "We need to get you to see a doctor." His hand moved to my stomach, which still appeared to be flat. His thumb gently moved over the skin and my belly button.

"I've been meaning to make an appointment, but I wanted to wait until you were better."

"I'm fine," he said. "I care more about making sure Little Barsetti is doing okay."

"I'm sure they're fine. If they're anything like us, they'll be indestructible."

He leaned down and pressed a kiss to my forehead. "You're probably right about that."

Chapter 15

ADELINA

I didn't know what to expect when he walked through the door.

He would be furious with me for tattling on him to Pearl. But I didn't have any other option. I was in a troubling situation, and Pearl and Crow were the only people who seemed to have any effect on him anymore.

His engine was loud as he entered the property and pulled into the driveway. He shut the door hard, and I could hear his approach through the walls of this beautiful house. A part of me wanted to run upstairs and hide in my bedroom, but there was no hiding from this man.

I was at his mercy.

I didn't mind the way he fucked me roughly because it felt good. I didn't mind it when he grabbed me and kissed me without giving me notice. But I didn't like the way our relationship had changed. It was like I wasn't a person anymore, just a body. I didn't like meaning nothing to him.

I wanted to mean something.

I stayed on the couch and listened to his footsteps grow louder. His keys clanked against the table when he tossed them on the surface. His wallet gave a gentle thud when he dropped it. His footsteps sounded again as he walked through the kitchen and entered the living room.

And then he was there.

Staring at me.

He looked at me on the couch, his arms resting by his sides with a leather jacket over his shoulders. His expression was impossible to read, but one thing was for certain.

He knew.

I kept my legs crossed and wore the same brave face I hadn't dropped. When Tristan was my captor, I never showed my fear. Cane wasn't any different.

After what felt like minutes, he moved to the couch beside me. He didn't touch me, didn't grab me by the back of the neck. He rested his arms on his knees and stared at the floor. His sunglasses were still on, so he pulled them off and tossed them on the table.

I was still, not letting my breathing escalate. I kept calm even though I didn't feel calm. I used to feel this tension whenever he was in the room, but it was for a completely different reason.

"Pearl told me you stopped by." He spoke quietly, not raising his voice or darkening his tone. He faced the TV but didn't look at it. His black watch was tight around his wrist, reflecting the flames in the hearth.

I didn't say anything, knowing the statement didn't need a response.

He sat back against the cushion but continued to face forward. "I was really angry, but both of them managed to talk me down."

He must be referring to Crow.

"And I've come to the realization that they are right. Just because I'm not getting my way doesn't mean I have the right to do this to you. If you were someone else and I didn't care about you, that would be different. But since I... feel this way...it's clouded my judgment. I used to be a horrible person, but I'm not that man anymore. That's something I'm proud of...and I can't go back."

My heart finally relaxed as his confession swept over me. He didn't see me as a prisoner anymore. He realized he'd lost himself in his emotions, and it was time to get back on track. I knew the Cane I adored was still in there, just buried under his sadness.

"I'll take you back to South Carolina whenever you're ready. Just tell me when." He stared at his hands, massaging his knuckles and his wrist. The jacket was tight across the muscles of his back and arms. His sculpted thighs were tight in his jeans. When he was in all black, he looked particularly handsome.

I wanted to say something because I'd been silent the entire time. But words were difficult to form. I was relieved he found his way back to where he belonged. I knew he would crawl out of this hole eventually.

"But I want to know something." He finally turned his head my way and locked his eyes on mine.

I felt a shiver up my spine when he looked at me that way, those green eyes burning into mine. His power was obvious in the look. He could make me feel so much and so little at the same time.

"I want to know exactly how you feel about me—the complete truth. Nothing you say will change my mind about returning you. I just want to know. I've been completely honest with you about the depth of my feelings, my love as well as my anger. I want the same from you."

"The way I feel?" I whispered.

"About me," he pressed.

I looked into his handsome features, the strong jaw as well as the hard expression on his face. His dark brown hair was soft even though it was short, and his slight stubble was growing thicker and darker by the hour. In just a few months, I'd come to know Cane in a way I'd never become acquainted with another man. He had a piece of me no one else would ever have. "When we first met, I felt something."

"What?" he whispered.

"I don't know. You seemed kind, handsome. When I saw you at the airport, I wished you were hitting on me in the past. Like, I was in a coffee shop on campus, and you decided to stop by for a chat. You were the kind of man I'd find attractive, despite how intimidating you were."

Cane listened to me, his eyes trained on my face.

"When I was Tristan's prisoner, he did horrible things to me. Not just him, other men did too. It was a terrible introduction to sex. It was painful and uncomfortable. No woman should have to go through it. And then when you came into that room, I wasn't so scared. I knew if I said no, you would listen…and you did. You were a breath of fresh air in the middle of a landfill. You kissed me when no other man had touched me like that…and I really liked it. I thought it was strange I could feel good when all I'd felt until that moment was utter terror. And then you took me as a loan…and I was relieved."

Cane's expression didn't change. He hardly blinked as he listened to me describe my opinion of our relationship.

"I thought I was fond of you because you were nice to me. But then I realized I loved the way you touched my hand, the way you looked at me like I was the only thing that mattered. You wanted to be with me, but you always let me have the final say in the matter. You told me I had no control, but you had given me all of it. I knew in the beginning that you were a good man. I knew you weren't like the others. You weren't exactly a saint, but you weren't a demon either. And when we had sex the first time…I really liked it." I remembered how good it felt, how he made me come so easily. It was my first orgasm during intercourse, and it was phenomenal. It was how every woman should feel during sex. "I wanted more. I wanted it every night. I wanted to sleep beside you because I hated being alone. You protected me, chased away all the nightmares."

He moved his arm over the back of the couch, and his hand slid into my hair, gently touching me behind the ear.

"And then you did the unthinkable…you rescued me. I never expected you to do that. When you dropped me off, I thought that was the last time I would ever see you. I pictured your face during the most difficult times because it made things easier. When you took me away from there, I had no words to describe your heroism. You gave up everything just to free me. You killed all his men and broke the chains around my ankle. You gave me a new start when I didn't think I'd ever have one. I thought I would die in that place, but you gave me new life. I'll never be able to thank you for doing that for me. I'm not sure what I did to deserve your affection. I'm a victim of rape and kidnapping—"

"You aren't a victim. You're a survivor. Don't look at yourself that way—I don't."

My eyes softened at the sweet words. "But still…I'm not exactly the ideal woman."

"I've never wanted ideal. I never knew what I wanted until I found you."

Now my heart softened, wilting like a plucked rose.

"What do you feel now?" he pressed. "After what I've done to you." It was the first time he looked away, like he was ashamed.

"I don't think less of you. I knew that wasn't the real you. I've seen your soul before, and that wasn't it."

He closed his eyes for a few seconds before he opened them again.

"I know I'll miss you when I leave, Cane. I know I'll think about you all the time. But I can't give up my life to stay here. Everything I've ever known has been left behind. If I do stay…Tristan wins. I was happy in South Carolina. I had my parents, friends, school…"

He shifted his gaze to the floor.

"I can't give all that up when I was never meant to leave. I was supposed to have a different destiny."

He didn't get angry like he did last time. He stayed exactly the same, quiet and somber. "You're sure you don't love me?"

The question hung in the air between us, making me feel sick all the way to my stomach. Something was burning at me from the inside, making me feel faint and weak. My lips could barely move. I wasn't sure if I could answer. "If I let myself love you, I'll never go back…and I have to go back."

He turned back to me, his eyes narrowing. "So you do love me…you just don't want to."

I refused to answer the question, to let the words fill the space between us. Once I did, there was no going back. If I stayed with Cane, I would never know what my life would have been like. Would I have met a nice guy who would be soft and gentle with me? Would I finally teach in a classroom and make an impact on young minds? If I hadn't been taken, where would I be right now? "As comfortable as it is here, I know it's not where I belong."

———————

I WASHED my face in the bathroom then retreated to my private room where all my things were. I had my own TV, a fireplace, and more space than necessary. Cane and I hadn't spoken since our intense conversation, and I'd stayed away from him. I couldn't tell if he was mad, hurt, or simply indifferent.

He came down the hall and knocked on my open door. He was in just his boxers, over six feet of muscle and man. He was barefoot and bare-chested, sexy and chiseled. Sometimes I wasn't sure if his face was more handsome than his body, or if it was the other way around. He was perfect. "You're welcome to sleep with me…if you'd like."

I was sitting on the bed with my legs crossed. His baggy shirt was loose over my shoulders, and my hair was smooth because I'd just brushed it after washing my face. My makeup was gone, so my face was washed out. "Do you want me to sleep with you?"

He leaned against the doorway, crossing his muscular arms over his chest. "Would I have asked if I didn't?"

"No…probably not."

"Then the ball is in your court." He left the door open and walked away.

I didn't like sleeping alone. I'd been sleeping alone my whole life and I used to like it, but after Cane and I shared a bed for a month, it was impossible to go back. I relied on his breathing like a sleeping pill. He protected me from my nightmares with his powerful presence. He could even guard me from my own subconscious.

It didn't take me long to find my answer.

I joined him in his bedroom, seeing the fire in the hearth and the beautiful man in the bed. The sheets were bunched around his waist as he looked at his phone. The light from the screen lit up his face as one of his arms was tucked beneath his head.

I got into bed beside him and pulled the sheets to my shoulder.

He set the phone on the nightstand then turned to me. "I was hoping you would come."

"I like sleeping with you."

"You do?"

"Yeah. I always sleep better."

He turned over in bed and faced me, his body staying on his side of the bed. "I sleep better too."

I looked into his eyes and saw him look back at me. When it was just the two of us, his expression wasn't so hard. He didn't seem like the solider that killed every man in his path just to get to me. He didn't seem like the ruthless barbarian that would do whatever he wanted until he got his way. He was just a man.

"I never apologized to you…"

"You don't need to apologize, Cane."

"I think otherwise."

"You've done so much for me...you've earned a pass."

The corner of his mouth rose in a smile. "A pass, huh?"

"Yeah."

"I wish my brother would give me one of those. Never does."

"Family is different. You're always forgiven, but you're always teased, too."

"True."

My hand slid across the sheets until I found his. My fingers explored the veins over his knuckles as they extended up his forearms. I loved the way his arms were sculpted. He was just muscle and bone, nothing else.

"When do you want to leave?"

The sudden question made me flinch. "I don't know..."

"It's up to you. I can book your flight whenever you want."

"You won't come with me?"

"I don't see why I would. It's not like your parents will be thrilled to see me."

"They don't hate you."

"They don't like me either. And they shouldn't like me."

He pulled his hand away and propped himself on his elbow. His hand snaked across the bed until he touched my thigh. His fingers tested my reaction, seeing if I wanted him or not.

My legs parted, giving him access between my legs.

His fingers slowly moved up until he reached my panties. He pulled aside my thong and pressed his thumb directly against my clitoris.

It made me gasp quietly.

He rubbed it gently, igniting the tenderness between my legs. The stimulation immediately made my mouth dry, made my back arch in pleasure. He touched me in just the right ways, making me shift and move.

I pulled my thong down my legs under the sheets and kicked it away so he would have access to all of me.

Two fingers slipped inside me, and he kept his thumb against my clitoris. He fingered me, feeling my channel become soaked from his touch. My breathing escalated, and my nipples turned hard like rocks.

He moved closer to me on the bed then leaned down to kiss me. His kiss was soft and wet, full of the passion he used to show me. His mouth guided mine, and he breathed into me, giving me his breath and taking mine away.

One of my hands snaked into his hair while the other wrapped around his neck. My legs were completely open to him now, so he could touch me whatever way he wanted. His thumb excited my clit further, pressing harder and harder until my hips started to buck.

I was just about to come. All I needed were a few more minutes. But I didn't want to come because of his hand. I wanted to come because his thick dick was inside me, making love to me like we used to every single night.

"Cane…make love to me." I spoke between his kisses, my eyes closed and my nails digging deep.

He kicked his boxers off then rolled his body on top of mine. My thighs were pushed back by his, and he slid inside me, pushing through my wet tightness until he was completely sheathed.

That was all I needed. I was already going to come. After a few thrusts, I clawed at his back and exploded around his dick, coming like I never had before. It was so powerful I forgot to breathe. I forgot everything in the world. All I thought about was the unbridled passion between us.

When I was finished, he smiled down at me. "That didn't take long."

My arms hooked around his neck, and I locked my ankles behind his back. "I'm sure it won't take long to do it again either."

Chapter 16

Cane

When I got off the phone with the soil specialist, I called Crow.

"Yes?"

"Uh, hi. Bitchy today?"

"I can't get Button in to see the doctor until tomorrow. Apparently, a hundred grand doesn't mean shit to him."

"Is she okay?" I blurted. "Why does she need to see a doctor?"

"Because she's pregnant—idiot."

"And that can't wait another day? Idiot."

"You know me, Cane. I'm paranoid about a lot of things."

"Crow, there's nothing to be paranoid about. She's, like, a month along. Nothing significant could happen in that amount of time."

"Until a doctor tells me everything is good, I'll be thinking about it."

"Then why didn't you take her sooner?"

"In case you've forgotten, my ribs were broken, and I couldn't walk."

"She could have gone by herself."

"I want to be there," he snapped. "This is my kid. I want to be there for everything."

I'd probably be the same way if I were in his shoes. "Then tomorrow isn't far away. Just chill."

"Why are you calling?" he blurted.

"I heard back from the soil specialist. He said the nitrogen is perfect, and the soil contains the perfect moisture levels. It's packed with other minerals too. So I'm going to close this deal unless you have a problem with it."

"What happened with Adelina?"

I sat back against my chair in my office. "What does she have to do with this?"

"When I tell Pearl I talked to you, she's gonna ask me. I need this information so I have something to relay back to her. What happened?"

"She and I are fine. Let's move on."

"No, I need more than that. Are you letting the woman go?"

I didn't want her to leave, but it wasn't right for me to make her stay. Maybe when she returned home, she would understand she'd outgrown the place. She wasn't the same person, so the place would never feel like home again. "Yes."

"Good. I'm glad you stopped being a dictator."

"Again, you're one to talk."

"Not the same thing."

"I disagree," I said. "So, are we moving forward on this property? I just need to know you're on board. I'll head down and take care of everything since I know you're busy."

"I think we should move forward."

"Awesome. I'll let you know how it goes." I hung up then left the office.

Adelina was in the living room reading. She watched me grab my keys and wallet from the table. "Are you leaving?"

"Yeah. Need to take care of business."

"When will you be back?"

I shoved my phone into my pocket. "A few hours. I'm buying that piece of land Crow and I talked about."

"Oh…can I come along?"

I grinned. "Why? Because you'll miss me?"

She smiled. "Would you judge me if I said yes?"

"No judgments, *Bellissima*."

———

WE HAD dinner on the terrace then retired to my bedroom on the top floor. The master was big with its own living room, bedroom, and an enormous bathroom. It was too big for two people. And it was far too big for one person.

We got into bed, and once our bodies were naked between the sheets, I was in between her legs. I was on top because I didn't want her any other way. I loved watching her lips tremble when I touched her in just the perfect way. I loved feeling how wet she was as I ground against her. She had the most perfect tits, and I loved watching them shake as I thrust.

I wasn't in the mood to fuck. Just to make love.

Making her come was the easiest thing in the world. She was receptive, sexual, and immensely attracted to me. She didn't think about the horrible things Tristan and his men did to her. When I was buried inside her, she only thought about me.

And she knew I would never hurt her.

I came inside her before I rolled off her, suddenly feeling depressed once we were done. My time with her was limited. Any day now, she would ask me to buy her a one-way ticket back home. My bed would be empty, and within a few weeks, her smell would disappear from my home.

And I would be alone.

I'd pick up women in Florence to fight the loneliness.

I'd think of Adelina as I fucked them.

And once enough time passed and I finally stopped thinking about Adelina, maybe I would try to find someone that I could share my life with. Being with Adelina made me realize that was exactly what I wanted—if I found the right person.

I wanted what Crow had.

I wanted a woman.

I wanted a family.

I wanted it to be Adelina—but I might not get my way.

A part of me believed she would return home and realize it wasn't the same anymore. She was too different, and everyone viewed her differently. They would view her as the victim, the person who'd been raped by a gang of thugs. She believed her life would be a fairy tale and Prince Charming would sweep her off her feet. But there was no Prince Charming.

The only man who would risk his life to save hers was me—and I already did.

But she had to realize it on her own.

And I had to hope that she came back to me.

I understood her stubbornness. I hadn't wanted to return Adelina to Tristan, but I did it anyway because I couldn't go back on my word. If Adelina never returned home to be with her friends and family, she would be betraying them. She wasn't selfish—and I respected that.

Adelina lay against me, her hand on my chest. She was curled into my side, her hair all over my chest and shoulder. I loved the way she smelled, especially when she smelled like me. Her eyes were closed, and she tucked her leg in between mine.

I looked at the ceiling as I ran my fingers through her

hair. I paid attention to the way she breathed, the way her chest rose and fell at a soft rate. Her eyelashes were dark and thick, hiding those beautiful eyes when she looked down. Her tits were soft against my chest. I loved caressing them with my fingertips and my lips.

She must have felt me staring at her because she opened her eyes and looked into my face. The gentle glow from the fire made her features visible. Without makeup and with swollen lips, she looked like the most beautiful thing in the world. "I think I should be getting home soon…"

My fingers halted in her strands, but I kept my expression the same. I knew she was wary of my reaction—not that I could blame her. "Pick a date."

"The longer I wait, the more my parents will suffer… and Lizzie's."

"I understand."

Chapter 17

CROW

"So, they're both okay?" I stared at the doctor, the most revered obstetrician in Europe. I flew Button all the way to France, a two-hour plane ride, just to see him. I wasn't letting her see anyone unless they were the best in the business. We'd have to make arrangements for when Button was ready to deliver. "Both healthy?"

"Based off of everything I've seen, they're both in great shape."

Button was still lying on the table in her gown, so I rested my hand on top of her stomach and felt the relief wash over me. All the stress of the past month hadn't harmed Little Barsetti. She'd told me she was pregnant in the middle of the storm, and all I could do was get both of them out of harm's way. But there had been nothing I could do to limit her distress. "I'm glad to hear that."

The doctor shook my hand before he stepped out of the room. "You're going to be a great father, Mr. Barsetti. I have a lot of concerned parents come into this room, but you lapped them by a mile." He smiled before he left.

Button was trying not to laugh. "If only he knew…"

I lifted up her gown and pressed a kiss to her belly, which was still flat. "Now I've got two people to look after. Stresses me out."

"Nothing to stress out about, Crow. This pregnancy will be boring. I'll get uncomfortable at the end and demand you retrieve me ice cream, but that's the worst of it."

"I hope so."

After she got dressed, we boarded my private plane and returned to Florence. It was a short trip when we cut out security. We landed in Florence, and I drove us back to the estate we both called home.

We walked inside and were greeted by Lars.

"How was the trip, Your Grace?" Lars retrieved my coat and hung it up by the door.

"Good," Button answered. "The baby is doing great. We won't know if it's a boy or a girl for a while, but they're healthy."

"That's great to hear," Lars said. "Lunch?"

"I'm starving," Button blurted as she rubbed her stomach.

"I could eat," I said simply.

"Great. Mr. Barsetti is waiting in the dining room for

you. I thought you could sit down to lunch together." Lars gave a slight bow before he walked away.

Cane was probably there to talk about business. He knew when I was going to be home and decided to bombard me right away. Being unemployed wasn't suitable for him. The only reason I put up with it was because I knew he was going through a hard time.

We walked into the dining room and found Cane enjoying a glass of wine.

"Coming around?" I asked as I sat across from him.

He took another drink then shrugged. "I guess. Not so bad."

Button sat beside me and helped herself to a fresh piece of bread. "How's the butler coming along?"

Cane swirled his wine around. "That man is a godsend. I understand your fascination with Lars."

"We aren't fascinated by him." I poured myself a glass of wine. "We just appreciate him."

"We should have our butlers battle and see who wins," Cane said. "My money is on Gerald."

"Are you kidding me?" Button asked. "Lars has served your family since you were born. He's put up with a ton of bullshit, so my money is on him. Gerald's patience will be tested the longer he works for you."

"True," Cane said. "I am a big pain in the ass. He likes Adelina, though."

"Because she's lovely." Button knew Cane was treating Adelina well, so she didn't ask any questions about it.

"How was the doctor?" Cane asked. "You guys are in good spirits, so I guess it went well?"

"Yeah," Button answered. "Crow was a little paranoid, but everything was fine."

"Why are you surprised?" Cane asked. "Crow is paranoid about everything."

"For a reason," I said coldly. Being paranoid saved my life a few times—and my wife's.

Button had a glass of water because that was all she could drink. "How are things going with Adelina?"

Cane suddenly looked miserable once the question was asked. "She's leaving on Friday. I bought her a ticket."

Button's face fell in sadness, and I was disappointed too. Adelina was a nice woman, and she complemented my brother well. But she deserved to be free like everyone else. If it was meant to be, she would come back to him. "I'm sorry, man."

Cane refilled his glass even though he hadn't finished it and drank more. "It's shitty. But there's nothing I can do."

"There's still hope," Button said. "There's always hope."

"I don't know," Cane said. "She was close with her parents. I know she wants to see them. And even if she wanted to come back, we can't have a future. Her parents hate me, as they should. Her friends will hate me. She would never leave them behind to stay with me, and I would never move there either. It's the definition of hopeless."

I couldn't contradict any of that logic. She would have to turn her back on the only life she'd ever known to live across the world. The trip was too far to receive visitors often. She might see her parents once a year. But they would never approve of her running off with a criminal like Cane. They would ask her to see a therapist before they let that happen.

"I didn't stay with Crow just because I had nothing else," Button said. "I stayed because it felt like home. When I was back in New York, everything felt the way it used to. I worked, walked down the same streets I'd always known, and ate at my favorite places. But it was too normal. Jason looked at me like I was damaged goods, about to fall apart right in front of him. Ordinary lives now seemed boring to me. I didn't belong there anymore. I think Adelina will see that. She'll be upset that she can't go back. But once she stops fighting it, she'll give in."

Cane sighed as he looked into his glass. "I hope so. She basically said she loves me but doesn't want to. She doesn't want to because she's not willing to give up everything to stay here with me. But I guess I understand…"

When it came to Button, I had her wrapped around my finger within a few months. She told me she loved me, but I was the one who pushed her away. Once I allowed my heart to truly cherish her, there was no going back. My soul had committed to her for the rest of my existence. Like it was etched in stone forever and permanent, I couldn't stop even if she asked me to. It didn't surprise me that Adelina refused to say it. Once she did, Cane wouldn't let her leave. And she wouldn't want to leave either. "You know we're here for you."

"Yeah," Cane said. "I know." He poured another glass of wine and downed it like water.

I eyed his movements. "Not piss anymore, huh?"

"I don't care at this point," Cane said. "I just need booze, and Lars wouldn't give me the good stuff."

———

BUTTON CAME up behind me as I pulled off my shirt and tossed it on the floor. Her hands moved down my back, feeling the lines of muscle on either side of my spine. She pressed a kiss to the center of my back, her fingers caressing me. "How do you feel?" Her hand moved over the incision point, where there was a faint scar.

"Fine."

"What about your ribs?"

"Hardly feel them anymore." It took me a while to get back on my feet. I still hadn't started running because I didn't want to push it, but I was finally able to get around the house and go back to work.

"Good." She kissed me again. "I'm glad you're feeling better."

"Enough about me." I turned slightly and looked over my shoulder at my small wife. Over a foot shorter than me with beautiful brown hair and a sexy curve to her hips, she was perfect. I'd been with women from all over the world, but not a single one compared to her. Button was perfect in so many ways that existed underneath the skin. She was the strongest person I knew, absolutely fearless, and she would do anything to protect me—just the way I would for her. "The only thing we need to be thinking about is Little Barsetti." My hand moved to her stomach over her shirt.

"Little Barsetti is fine, so we don't need to worry there. And is that what we're going to keep calling them?"

"Yeah."

She smiled. "It's cute. Do you have any real names in mind?"

"No." I'd only just grasped the idea that, in a few months, it wouldn't be just the two of us anymore. I imagined a baby, not necessarily a boy or a girl. I was going to be a father, and that meant my paranoia would reach new heights. "Do you?"

"Actually, yes. If it's a girl…Vanessa."

I stilled at her words, feeling her fingertips still touching me. The name brushed over my skin and elicited memories I would never forget. Cane and I teased Vanessa all the time when we were growing up, but we were also immensely protective of her. On her first date, we'd threatened to rip the guy's throat out and then dig out everything else. Sometimes I thought about her, and it was always with a twinge of sadness. I missed her.

I slowly turned the rest of the way around and came face-to-face with Button. "Vanessa, huh?"

"What do you think?" she whispered. "Would be a nice way to keep her around…"

My fingers moved underneath her chin, and I directed her gaze higher, making her lock eyes with me. "You would do that?" I was certain Button had different names she loved, but she knew how important my sister was to me— even if I never mentioned her. It shouldn't surprise me that Button would offer something like this. She did a lot for me —things I took for granted.

"Of course. I think it would be nice. Do you like it?"

"I love it." My palm moved to her cheek, feeling the soft and delicate skin. A hint of blush was in her face, contrasting against those pretty blue eyes.

"Then it's settled. All you need to do is check with Cane."

"Why would I check with him?"

"Maybe he was planning on naming his daughter Vanessa."

"Let's not jump the gun. I wouldn't be surprised if he never had kids."

"There's hope…"

"There's always hope. But that doesn't mean it'll happen."

———

I SAT in my study and went through the files left on my computer. My client list was still up to date from the weapons business. I had every name, rendezvous point, and unlimited details about the people I did business with. It didn't make sense keeping it all, so I considered deleting it.

But that wasn't so easy.

I wasn't as attached to the business as Cane was. I was only a partner because he asked me to be one. It was a monster too big for a single person to tackle, so having both of us made it a lot easier. But I didn't like the association it had with my father.

I didn't hate my father, but I didn't exactly respect him either.

I never cared that he made his money in criminal ways. It was the reason I had clothes on my back and food on the table. It was the reason I lived in a three-story mansion surrounded by vineyards and countryside.

But I cared about the way he'd treated my mother. He screwed other women on his own time, took advantage of women who didn't have any rights. My mother knew about the cheating, but that never stopped my father.

He betrayed his family.

That was why I didn't respect him.

No matter what obstacles would come our way, I would never do that to my wife. I would never take another woman and rip her apart. Button was my life, and she deserved nothing but my full commitment. Occasionally, I wanted something darker, to make marks on her skin with my whip, but I certainly wouldn't run off and get it somewhere else.

Saying goodbye to this business wasn't difficult for me. It was time for it to come to an end.

It was time for Cane and me to make our own legacy, to make the Barsetti name mean something new. I was starting a family, and now I was living a civilian life with civilian rules. I still had guns stashed around the house, and I would never stop looking over my shoulder, but everything needed to change.

Hopefully, Cane would realize that. If he had Adelina to settle down with, that could have been a possibility.

Unfortunately, it wasn't.

A light knock sounded on my door before Button opened it. She saw me sitting at my desk, a decanter of scotch and a glass of ice cubes prepared for me to enjoy. I was drinking again because nothing else would quench my thirst for scotch. I'd known it was my drink since the first time I had it at sixteen.

She slowly approached my desk, wearing one of my black t-shirts that reached her knees. She eyed the amber liquid on my desk but didn't swat me on the nose for it. She hopped up on the edge of the desk and rested her feet on my thigh.

My hand circled around her calf, feeling her smooth legs.

"What are you doing in here?" Her legs were slightly parted, revealing the black thong she wore underneath the shirt.

I shut the laptop and grabbed my drink. "Just some work."

"What kind of work?"

"Going through our old clients. Constantine must have made it clear we were no longer associated with the business but everything would run just as smoothly."

She tilted her head to the side, watching me with her knowing gaze. "Are you alright with that?"

"Yes."

"You're sure about that?" She picked up on my moods like she could feel them through her skin.

I took a drink before I set the glass down. "I understand why Cane has such a hard time with it. It belonged to our family. Now it belongs to someone else. It was our legacy, something one Barsetti handed down to another. Now I have my own Barsetti coming along...makes me think of what I'll leave them when I'm gone."

"Why are we thinking about that?" she asked. "You and I will both be around for a very long time."

"I know. Just makes me wonder what kind of legacy I want to build. Cane and I can have the wine business. It's honorable. It's clean."

"It doesn't break the law," she said with a smile.

"So perhaps this can be our new legacy. Maybe the Barsettis can have a new start. Maybe we can be remembered for something else."

"Exactly," she said. "I think that sounds great."

"I hope Cane agrees. I know losing the business and losing Adelina have been difficult for him."

"When the baby comes, he'll have something to look forward to." She crossed her legs and leaned forward, staring down at me. "And Adelina will come back."

"We don't know that."

"I think she will."

"They aren't us, Button," I whispered.

"No, they aren't. But she and I are the same. There's no going back after what we've been through. No one will ever understand. No one will ever know how to treat us. Only you and Cane seem to get it. She'll realize that—and then she'll come back."

Chapter 18

ADELINA

After I packed my bags, we put them in the car then drove away from the house.

I stared at it the entire time until it was completely gone from sight. I wanted to remember the stone walkway, the cobblestone walls, the large furnace in the front of the house. I wanted to remember the roses right out front, the large Mediterranean windows that overlooked the acres of property he owned. I'd never forget the view out my bedroom. Looking out was the first thing I did every single morning.

Now I would never see it again.

Cane was silent on the drive, one hand on the wheel while the other rested on the gearshift. He wore all black, his signature look. He didn't seem upset by my departure, but his feelings were hidden underneath that stoic expression. The radio was off, so it was just the two of us in tension-filled silence.

I didn't know what to say since it was painful for both of us. Goodbye was too difficult. And to make small talk like nothing was happening was insulting. So I didn't say anything back, my eyes focused out the window.

He grabbed my hand and interlocked our fingers while his eyes remained glued to the road.

I refused to let myself cry.

Twenty minutes later, he arrived at the international airport. He pulled over into a spot right at the terminal and put it in park. People unloaded their cars and passengers walked through the automatic doors so they could catch their flights. Everyone had somewhere to go, all in a hurry.

Cane stared forward until he opened the glove box and pulled out a stack of paperwork. "Here's your ticket." He set it in my lap. "I arranged for a car to pick you up. They'll take you wherever you want to go."

"Thank you." He'd already done so much for me, and even now, he was still taking care of me.

He handed me more paperwork. "I opened an account in your name in America. It has enough to get you whatever you need."

"What does that mean?" I flipped through the pages until I found the deposit information. "Cane…" He'd put hundreds of thousands of dollars into my account. "Why? You didn't need to do that…"

"I want you to have what you need. You can go back to

school without worrying about money. You can buy your-self a house. It's one less thing to stress about."

Tears started to burn my eyes. "You don't owe me anything, Cane."

"I know," he said quietly. "I just...I want you to be taken care of."

I took a shaky breath and felt the tears stream down my face. "I can't accept this."

"Yes, you can. This money is nothing to me. I would much rather you have it than hold on to it. It'll make transi-tioning so much easier."

"But I don't want you for your money, Cane. That's not why—"

He grabbed the papers and put them back together for me in an envelope. "I know." He placed the debit card in my hand. "But you're going to need to buy lunch. You know you need to eat every hour."

No joke in the world could make me laugh right now.

"I'm not taking it back, so you may as well keep it." He got out of the driver's seat and opened the trunk. He pulled out my luggage on wheels and placed it on the sidewalk, the handle pulled up.

It took me a second to get out of the car and to wipe away the tears that had fallen down my cheeks. I fixed my makeup and realized we were at the airport where I saw Cane for the very first time. Now it might be the last time I ever saw him.

I got out of the car and met him on the sidewalk.

His features were exactly the same. He didn't shed a single tear or show any emotion. It didn't seem like we were saying goodbye. It didn't seem like he loved me, as if he'd never told me those words in the past.

I was the one who wanted to leave, but I was the one crying.

He cupped my face with both hands and wiped the new tears away with his thumbs.

"I can't thank you enough for everything you've done for me. If it weren't for you, I would still be there…or I would be dead."

He stepped into me and kissed me on the forehead. "I would do it again if I had to, *Bellissima*."

I would miss that name. *Bellissima*. I rested my face against his chest and hugged him, knowing I would miss the way he felt in my arms. His cologne washed over me, making me think of long nights when we didn't get any sleep. Those memories would comfort and hurt me in the years to come.

Cane pulled away and looked down into my face. "I want to say something."

"Okay."

"Home might not be what you remember. You've changed so much that it might not feel the same. People will treat you differently. What used to be simple and beautiful might now be completely different. You aren't the same person, and neither are they. You'll try to have a normal life. You'll try to be around people again, date guys again…

but it won't be what you expect. I think you'll come to realize that I'm the only one who truly understands you. I'm the only one who won't think less of you for what you've endured. I'm the only one who will admire you for what you've suffered."

I felt the truth of his words and feared he was right. Home might not be what I remembered. People might see me as the woman who was sold into sex trafficking the second she graduated college. I would be recognized everywhere. I wouldn't have a clean start.

"No matter how much time has passed, if you ever want to come back, my door will be open." He pulled out a cell phone from his pocket and handed it to me. "My number is in there if you ever need anything…or if you just want to talk."

"Thank you." I held the phone in my palm and tucked it into my front pocket.

"You should get going."

"Okay…" All I had to do was grab my suitcase and walk away, but I didn't want to turn my back on him. I didn't want this to be the last time we saw each other. If he didn't live so far away, we could still see each other.

"Go, *Bellissima*." He cupped my face and kissed me on the mouth, a soft kiss that was heavy with a painful goodbye.

I kissed him back, treasuring the feel of his lips against mine. I would never forget this man for as long as I lived. He was an angel in a crowd of demons. He'd lost his temper for a few days, but he found himself once again.

He pulled away and pressed another kiss to my forehead. "I'll always love you, *Bellissima*." He turned away without looking at me again, making sure he got into his car without turning his face in my direction. The engine was on, and then he was on the road. He left the terminal and got lost in the sea of cars that were leaving the airport.

It was the first time I was truly alone since I'd been captured. I stood at the airport with my suitcase and more money than I could ever spend. I was a free woman. I could get on a plane to America, or I could get on a plane somewhere else. It didn't matter.

I was free.

Chapter 19

PEARL

"Leave him alone." Crow filled the door with his impressive size so I couldn't get by. "I know my brother. He just wants to be alone."

I pushed him aside, but he didn't move, much like a mountain. "No one wants to be alone."

"Men do." His hand moved to my arm, but he didn't grab me. Instead, he gently guided me away from the door. "Give him space."

I turned back around. "He needs a friend. He needs someone to talk to."

"I'm telling you, he doesn't want to talk right now."

"Well, if it were me, I'd want to talk to someone." I crossed my arms over my chest and looked up at my giant of a husband. "Now step aside, or I'll make you."

He didn't move.

"Why don't you want me to go? I'll only be gone for a few hours."

"I like it when you're home."

"Well, I'm needed right now."

"I guess I'll come with you, then."

"No." I grabbed my jacket off the coatrack. "He needs to talk to a woman. He'll say things to me that he won't say to you."

"And I don't want to hear them. We both know I'm not big on words."

"Yes." I rolled my eyes. "I'm aware."

"But I still think you should give him space. He's probably drunk."

"Drunk or not, he needs a friend." This time, Crow let me get to the door. I opened it then pulled out the keys I'd found on his nightstand. "By the way, you need to take me shopping. I need my own car."

"What do you need a car for?"

"Is that a serious question?" I asked. "I have to drive the kids to school, to soccer—"

"Lars can do it."

I pointed into his chest. "You do realize your enemies are gone, and there's nothing to be afraid of, right? And you do realize that I can't stay home all day and be a mother at the same time, right? I'm gonna be one of those soccer moms who's involved in everything and drives them crazy. So, I need a car, Crow."

He only wore a dark expression as a reaction.

I ignored it. "I'll be back."

"Text me when you get there, and text me when you leave."

I wanted to tell him off and say that was never going to happen, but after everything we'd been through, I thought his request was fair. "Alright."

He gripped me by the waist and kissed me hard on the mouth. "I love you, Button."

And as if we hadn't bickered back and forth for the past five minutes, I melted for this man. A part of me wanted to stay and curl into his lap for the rest of the night. We would lie in bed, and he would rub his large hand over my stomach, feeling the baby even though there wasn't much to feel. "I love you too."

———

I KNOCKED A FEW TIMES, but Cane didn't answer.

So I rang the doorbell several times.

A man I didn't know answered the door. He was in his late fifties, and he had dark hair that was perfectly combed back. He wore a collared shirt and slacks. "Can I help you?" He was rigid like Lars, standing perfectly straight with a welcoming smile on his lips.

"I'm Pearl Barsetti. I'm here to see Cane. You must be Gerald."

He shook my hand. "I'm glad he talks about me."

"Could you tell him I want to see him?"

"He's been upstairs all day. I haven't seen him once."

"He hasn't even eaten?" I asked with concern.

"I left a tray outside his door. Not sure if he was interested."

I'd known Cane would take Adelina's absence hard. The woman he loved wanted to start her life over where she was from. She didn't see a future where he could be in it too. "I need to see him. I'm very worried about him."

"I can let him know you're here and see what he says."

"He'll tell me to leave."

Gerald shrugged. "Then there's nothing I can do for you."

I wasn't leaving until I got an audience with my brother-in-law. "Gerald, I know you're new around here, so I'm going to go easy on you. But in situations like this, I get my way. I know Cane needs me even if he won't admit it. He's just going to stay locked up in his room drinking until somebody helps him back on his feet. So, are you going to continue standing in my way, or are you going to let me pass?"

He didn't think twice before he stepped to the side. "Come on in."

"Good choice, Gerald." I made my way upstairs and approached the master bedroom. The door was shut, so I knocked loudly against the wood. "Cane, it's me."

A growl sounded from the other side of the door. "What do you want?"

"You know what I want. Make yourself presentable because I'm about to open this door and walk in."

"Give me a second." He moved about the room, probably changing his clothes and cleaning up the beer and liquor bottles. A few minutes later, he opened the door himself, wearing a sour look and a thick beard. He turned away from the door and dropped onto the couch that faced the fireplace and enormous TV on his wall. His hair was flat like he hadn't showered since yesterday, and he looked thinner even though it'd only been a day since he'd last eaten, judging by the full tray sitting outside his door.

I sat beside him and stared at the sorrow in his eyes. He and Crow possessed some of the same expressions. They had the same smile, similar angry looks, and when they were devastated, they had the same matte look to their eyes.

"Why are you here?" he asked as he ran his fingers through his hair.

"You know why, Cane."

He rested his arm over the back of the couch and looked at the TV with sleepy eyes, like he'd had too much booze and wasn't in complete possession of his faculties. "There's nothing to say, so I'm not sure what we should do now."

"Have you talked to her since she left?"

He shook his head. "No."

"Does she have a number to call you?"

"I gave her everything she needs. I set up an account in her name, too. Wanted to make sure she'd have enough to get settled. I don't know what her plan is, but I assume she'll go straight to her parents' house first. But after that, I want her to be able to buy a house and not stress about money. From what I understand, teachers don't make much…"

The gesture was touching, but I shouldn't be surprised by his generosity. Cane had only loved one woman, and of course, he was going to make sure that one woman had everything she needed. "That was sweet."

"She almost didn't take it. But I asked her to."

"I think she'll come back, Cane."

"I hope." He covered his face with his hand then pinched the bridge of his nose. "Leaving her at the airport was a lot harder than I expected. Driving off and not looking back…felt strange. I wanted to call her and check on her after she landed, but I knew I couldn't. I know I need to leave her alone and let her get on with her life."

"It'll get easier," I whispered.

"No, it won't," he said as he shook his head. "In time, it'll be easier for me to lie to myself and say she didn't mean anything to me, but that's it. These feelings…this pain… won't go away. I feel the same way Crow felt when you were gone…unbearable agony." He dropped his hand then looked at the TV again.

"Did she say anything at the airport?"

"She cried. She thanked me for saving her. Said she would miss me." His eyes glazed over as he remembered

216

her parting words. "I told her I loved her then walked away. That's it."

"Then it was over?"

"Yeah," he whispered.

I hoped she would arrive in America and realize she wanted to come back, but I knew that was unrealistic. Once she tied up her loose ends, she would realize nothing was keeping her there. "She'll come back, Cane."

"I don't think so."

"She will. Just give it time."

He grabbed the half-full beer sitting on the table and took a drink. "Want anything?"

"I'm pregnant. I can't drink."

"Oh...that's right." He took another drink. "How's that going?"

"About the same. I don't feel any different."

"How's Crow been doing?" he asked. "Since we handed everything over to Constantine?"

"He's been good. He's been going to work and getting around the house. Hasn't started exercising yet, but he's almost there."

Cane leaned back and stared at the TV. "I feel like I've lost everything..."

I shifted my gaze back to his expression, seeing the powerful forlornness.

"That business meant everything to me. I don't blame Adelina, and I don't blame Crow... I don't blame anyone. I just feel lost without it. My dad built that thing from the ground up, and with the snap of a finger, it's gone." He shrugged. "And now, my woman is gone. Not sure who I am anymore."

"Crow talked to me about it the other day."

"About the business?" he asked.

"Yeah. He said he thought you guys were building a new legacy, a new future for the Barsettis. He said he was excited about it. Losing the business didn't feel like such a personal loss for him since there's so much more for you to do. He wants you to see it that way—as a new beginning, not an end."

Cane considered the words, his mouth heavy in a frown. "I know he's right. It's just hard for me to accept. He's good with change. I'm not."

"And Adelina will come back."

He stared at the TV. "Just because you did doesn't mean she will."

"I think so. It might take her a few weeks to figure it out, but I know she will."

He held the beer on his thigh and rubbed his thumb across the mouth. Back and forth, he moved, fidgeting quietly. "It was nice of you to come all the way down here to talk to me. You didn't have to do that."

"I wanted to."

"I'm a lucky guy. So is Crow. He can have you deal with me so he doesn't have to." He chuckled quietly, but his heart wasn't in it.

"He's worried about you, but he thought you wouldn't want to talk right now."

"He's right. I don't want to talk right now." He turned his gaze back to me. "But it doesn't feel so bad when I talk to you. Kinda reminds me of the way I used to talk to Vanessa. You know, she was the one member of our family who could humanize me. I wanted to be a better person because she looked up to me. I felt that way toward Adelina too...wanted to be a better man for her."

My hand reached for his.

He squeezed my fingers back. "Crow would be so jealous if he saw us right now."

"Crow is always jealous, so it doesn't matter."

"He should be jealous. I have the best sister in the world. That's something he doesn't have." He gave me a slight smile, the best he could do with the pain he was in.

I smiled and rested my head on his shoulder. "And I have the best brother in the world."

Chapter 20

ADELINA

My parents couldn't believe their eyes when I arrived on their doorstep.

They were in shock.

They were in tears.

And they could barely stand.

I was welcomed back into their home, and like I was a child all over again, my mother slept in my bed with me because she didn't want to be apart from me. Like I might slip away again, she hung on to me tightly.

The next day, the news media was there to interview my parents. Apparently, my story had gotten a lot of coverage since my parents hired so many private investigators to track me down. Lizzie's parents did the same, making us some of the most recognizable people in the United States.

I had no idea.

Giving the horrible news to Lizzie's parents was the hardest thing I'd ever had to do. I felt guilty for surviving when she had a terrible death. I couldn't even tell them where her body was so they could have a funeral. They cried—and I cried too. They said they were happy to see me, but I knew any parent would be devastated that I came back when their daughter never did.

Time seemed to move in slow motion, but everything was going so fast. The police interviewed me a few times and asked me the details of what happened. I told them the truth, but I kept Crow's and Cane's identities a secret. I told them Tristan and his men were dead, so there was no need to continue the investigation.

I got a lot of requests for interviews on daytime talk shows, but I declined all of them. The world was curious to know the things I had suffered, but I wasn't interested in sharing. The details weren't appropriate for television anyway. I didn't want my parents to have to listen to those tales.

I spent the first week at my parents' house. My old bedroom was exactly how I left it. They didn't change a single thing or throw anything out. When I was going to college, I still lived with them because it saved money. The college was down the road so I didn't need to commute far, but it was jarring living with them again.

I used to live with a gorgeous man in a mansion that I had all to myself most of the time.

My parents breathed down my neck, constantly asking I

needed anything or if there was something that would make me more comfortable.

I knew they meant well, so I didn't get irritated about it.

I was having dinner with them when my mother asked about Cane. "That man who brought you here a few months ago..."

My dad stared at his food, blocking out the conversation.

"Yeah?" I said.

"He was the one who set you free?" she asked.

"Yeah." I picked at my corn and mashed potatoes. "He is the one who killed Tristan and his men. He got me out of there, took care of me, and put me back together. He wanted me to stay with him, but I told him I had to get home."

"So, he's a criminal, but he still saved you?"

"Yeah," I answered. "Pretty much."

"Why would he do that for you?" she asked. "Why would that man go to such lengths to get you your freedom?" Mom was thinner than she used to be, having lost at least twenty pounds. It was most obvious in her face. She set her fork down and stared at me. "I wanted to ask before, but I didn't want to bombard you with questions."

There was no better way to explain it than by telling the truth. "He said he was in love with me..."

My dad looked up from his food.

"Oh," Mom said. "I see..."

"How do you feel about him?" Dad asked.

Dad had never asked me about something like that before. We never talked about boys. All topics related to sex were for my mother to handle. "I really care about him. He became a really good friend to me. I miss him…"

"Do you love him?" Mom pressed.

"I…I don't know." I looked down at my food again. "Everything that happened was so intense and fast. I'm not sure how I feel about it. I think he's a wonderful man, and I'll never be able to repay him for what he's done for me. But I don't understand how I feel about him beyond that. At the end of the day, he's still not exactly what I imagined in a boyfriend…or husband."

"You never answered the question," Mom said. "But I think that led you to your answer."

My heart stilled in my chest, stunned by her observation.

"I would love to speak with him, if you'd let me," Mom said.

"Why?" I asked.

"I need to thank him for bringing you back to us," she whispered. "I know the world is full of dark and dangerous men. He could have been like all the rest and left you to your fate. Even if his own motivations were sinister, he sacrificed a lot for you. He did the right thing when it came down to it. He deserves my gratitude."

I couldn't believe my ears.

Dad nodded in agreement.

"I guess I could call him tomorrow," I said. "It's really early in the morning there."

Mom glanced at the clock. "I'm sure he wouldn't mind."

"Uh…" I fought the urge to call him because I didn't want to play with his emotions. I didn't want to give him hope that I would come back if I wasn't sure I would. "Okay." I pulled out my phone and found his name in the phone book. It was the only name listed. I hit send.

He picked up immediately. *"Bellissima."* He spoke without emotion, sounding the same as he did when he dropped me off at the airport.

"Hey." I lost my train of thought when I heard his voice. I was brought back to the nights where he said that name in bed. "Uh, my mom wants to talk to you. I know that sounds weird, but…is that okay?"

If he was disappointed, he didn't indicate it. "Of course. I can listen to them yell at me."

"They don't want to yell at you. They want to thank you."

"Oh…" Cane turned quiet, considering what I'd said. *"Bellissima?"*

"Yeah?"

"Call me later when you have some privacy."

"Okay…I will." I handed the phone to my mom.

She took it and rested her elbows on the table. "Cane, right?"

Cane confirmed for her over the line.

"I wanted to thank you for rescuing my daughter." She'd hardly said a few words before her voice broke with emotion, the tears cascading. "She told me what happened. She told me that you accepted her as a loan, but then you did so much to save her…that you killed the man who took her and reclaimed her freedom. I don't know how I could ever thank you for what you did. You could have easily forgotten about her, but you didn't. I'm so glad you love her just as much as we do…so grateful."

I couldn't watch my mother cry anymore. It was too heartbreaking. I shifted my gaze away and stared down at my food.

———

WHEN MY PARENTS went to sleep, I called him from my bedroom. I was under the covers, wearing one of the t-shirts I stole from his drawer. It was a million sizes too big, but it still held his scent. It was faint, probably because it'd been smothered against all my other clothes during the journey underneath the plane.

He answered immediately. *"Bellissima."*

I closed my eyes as his voice swept over me like a gentle breeze in summer. "Yes."

"Where are you?" he asked.

"I'm in my old bedroom."

"You're staying with your parents?"

"Yeah…I was living here during college. I wanted to

save money while I went to school since it's right down the road. It's a free place to live with free food."

He chuckled. "That's cute."

"And…I kinda like living here. I've always been close with my parents."

"That's cute too," he said. "You know I don't like to be more than five miles away from Crow at any given time… even though I don't admit it."

I chuckled. "Yeah, I figured that out."

He fell quiet, staying on the phone in silence.

"What are you doing?"

"I'm sitting on the couch."

"Where?"

"In our bedroom." He sighed when he realized the error of his words. "My bedroom…"

I felt his pain seep through the phone. I could feel his misery surround me. I used to sleep in this bed every single night, but now I couldn't sleep well without him beside me. The mattress felt foreign. "I haven't been sleeping well. It's not the same without you."

"No, it's not," he whispered.

"Are you looking at the fireplace?"

"Yeah."

"What time is it there?"

"Early."

"Are you going to the winery?"

"No." He didn't elaborate, like he didn't want to share

any aspect of his life. "How are things there? I've seen you on the news a lot."

"You've been watching?"

"Yeah. You look beautiful in that red top, by the way."

"Thanks…" It was one of the first things Cane had bought for me. "It's been chaotic lately. I'm sure, in another week, everyone will move on to the next news cycle. I told Lizzie's parents…they were heartbroken."

"It must have killed them, but now they know what happened. They can make their peace with it."

"Yeah…"

"Your parents seem happy."

"They're…" There were no words. "I can tell it's been hard for them."

"I can only imagine. I only knew you for a few months, and I fell head over heels… Imagine how they feel when they've known you since the day you were born."

Every time he said those sweet things, I wanted to get on a plane and head back to him.

"What's next for you?" he asked. "Are you going to keep living there?"

"No, after living with you, it hasn't been easy going back to this. I'm gonna find an apartment soon. I just want to give my parents a little more time to have me in the house."

"You should be able to buy a nice house with the money I gave you. A good investment."

"Yeah…I'll think about it." I didn't want to buy

anything when I didn't know where I would be living. I wasn't quite sure where I wanted to settle down. "I need to complete another year of school before I can start teaching. I have to focus on that."

"You still want to be a teacher, huh?"

"Yeah."

"I think you'll be great at it. The kids will love you."

Talking to him was the easiest thing in the world. It was natural and so smooth. Talking to everyone else was jarring and painful. I didn't have to talk about Tristan with Cane. We could talk about so many other things because he didn't see me as some woman who was raped. He saw me as a person, along with all of my other qualities. "How are Pearl and Crow?"

"Crow is getting a lot better. He went for a run the other day and said he felt good."

"That's great."

"Pearl has been having some morning sickness. But she says it's not so bad."

"That's nice… Do they have names picked out?"

"Not that I know of," he said.

"What do you think they'll have?"

"A boy."

"Yeah?" I asked. "Why do you think that?"

"My father was one of five brothers. My parents had two boys. I just think we're a boy kinda family."

"Are you excited?"

"I'm very excited to be an uncle. I'm gonna piss off Crow by giving them candy, caffeine, and booze."

I chuckled, keeping my voice down so my parents wouldn't hear me. "He's gonna kill you."

"He's tried before, and it's never worked. I'm not scared."

"Well, I'm scared for you."

"Pearl will protect me. She tends to do that."

"You're lucky."

Once we ran out of things to say, we sat on the phone in silence. I couldn't hear anything on his end, and I wondered what the weather was like. Was it a sunny day? Was it rainy? Were his boxers on the floor where he always left them?

"I should let you go, *Bellissima*," he whispered. "It's late, and you must be tired."

"I am tired…" I closed my eyes as I sat on the phone.

Cane didn't hang up. He sat there with me, saying nothing.

I knew I shouldn't say it, but I wanted to say it anyway. I felt it deep in my chest. "I miss you…"

Cane took a deep breath. I could barely hear it over the line.

Before he had the chance to say it back, I ended the call. I tucked the phone under my pillow and tried not to think about him. I never should have said those words to him, but I couldn't help it. They slipped out like I had no control over my own behavior.

My eyes closed, picturing him as if he were right beside me. I pictured that smug smile, that brightness in his dark eyes, and I imagined how his hard chest felt against my hand. I quickly slipped away, disappearing into a deep sleep.

Chapter 21

CROW

We met with the contractors and got the permits so we could begin construction. We knew exactly where we would create the warehouses and the main building. It would be similar to my winery, so people would know they were related. Cane and I both wanted the same architectural style as my winery, so that meant cobblestone pathways, stone walls, and large windows that let in a lot of natural light. It would be a fine piece of Italian culture, something tourists would take pictures of if they drove by.

When the meeting was over, Cane and I entered the warehouses, and I went over the things that needed to be done. Since he needed something to do, I let him handle all the shipping and accounting. We had lots of barrels to keep track of, and we needed to give big clients the attention that they craved.

Cane was easy to work with. When we focused on the task at hand, he didn't seem so miserable. He was distracted enough so he didn't think about Adelina. Seeing him move around and get stuff done brought some life back into him.

He hadn't been this down since Vanessa.

And his response was exactly the same—to stay busy.

We walked up to the storage area for barrels that were packed with red wine. "We have regular big shipments to our biggest vendors in Florence and Rome. Most of our resources are used to fill these orders. Having that second location will be helpful since our production is maxed out right now."

Cane nodded in agreement. "Makes sense."

We walked through the warehouse then returned to the main building where my office was. My assistant had been working for me for years. She was a mother of three, and she liked having a low-stress job because her life was focused on being with her family. She never had any encounter with my illegal activities, and she had no idea who I truly was.

We walked past her and entered my office.

Cane sat across from my desk and rested one ankle on the opposite knee. "Everything seems pretty straightforward. So, you want me to manage the property?"

"I think it's a good idea. That way, when the other winery is done, you'll know exactly what to do. Besides, I could use the help around here anyway." Now that Pearl was having our first kid, she was my priority. I wanted to be there for her when she needed me. Work would come second now that my family was growing. I couldn't just put someone else in charge when I couldn't monitor them, but with Cane, I didn't need to worry about that.

"I think I got everything down. I wonder how long it'll be before the winery is finished."

"At least a year, unfortunately."

"I could still start the crop process. I'll have to haul everything back and forth, but at least we'd have more grapes for pressing."

"True."

He nodded then tapped his fingers against the wood of the armrests. His eyes scanned my office, seeing the paintings on the wall and the picture I had of Pearl on our wedding day. His eyes sat there for a long time before he finally looked out the window.

I could see the misery written across his face. "How are you?"

"A little overwhelmed but I'll get into the swing of things. I'm smarter than you give me credit for."

"I wasn't asking about work," I said quietly.

Cane's eyes shifted to me, knowing exactly what I was referring to.

I hated putting my brother on the spot, but I couldn't ignore his devastation. No matter how hard he tried to hide it, I could see it.

"There's nothing to say," he said. "I'm fine."

"You don't seem fine."

He shrugged. "Okay, I'm not fine. But it doesn't change anything. No need to talk about it."

"Have you spoken to her?"

"The other day, actually."

I couldn't hide my surprise. I'd assumed she would never call him, and he had too much pride to call her. "What happened?"

"She called me because her mom wanted to speak to me."

"And what did she say?"

His eyes shifted to the picture of Pearl and me again. "She thanked me for rescuing Adelina and returning her home." He spoke without emotion, like the memory of the conversation meant nothing to him. "Later, Adelina called me when she was in her bedroom. We talked for a little while, about her life and the attention she was getting. When we got off the phone...she told me she missed me then hung up."

Adelina didn't seem like someone who would just say something without meaning it. She wouldn't torture Cane for no reason. "Pearl was right. She'll come back."

He released a heavy sigh that was burdened with sadness. "I hope so. Talking to her just...makes me miss her even more. I try to stay busy so I don't think about her, but when I'm in my bedroom at night...it's hard not to." Instead of projecting his tough-guy image, Cane was vulnerable with me. He obviously didn't care what anyone thought of him anymore.

"She'll come back, Cane. She'll realize she doesn't belong there."

"I don't know…"

"You could always go there and see her."

He shook his head. "No. I'm not going to do that. I'd be invading her space."

"You could just say you were in town and ask her to dinner or something. No pressure."

Cane stared at the picture frame in silence.

"I wish I could help you, Cane. I don't like seeing you like this."

His eyes turned back to me, and the affection emerged in his eyes. "I know. I don't know what to do. I'm usually aggressive and just take what I want, but that won't work for me now. Everything I've ever learned in my life doesn't apply here."

"Yeah, it seems that way."

"A part of me wishes I'd never fallen for her. Another part wouldn't have it any other way."

I left my desk and opened the cabinet. I poured two glasses of scotch and handed one to him. "Our lives used to be so much easier before the women came."

He chuckled then took a drink. "I'll drink to that."

"But I know what you mean. I wouldn't want it any other way." I drank from my glass and watched my brother on the other side of the desk. "I used to hate sharing my space, but now I hate it when Pearl isn't sleeping beside me. I used to enjoy my solitude, but I hate it when we aren't together, even for a few hours. Now I'm dependent on this woman for my happiness. It's scary sometimes."

He looked down into his glass with a sad expression. "I know that feeling…all too well."

———

WHEN I CAME HOME, Button was on the third floor, but she wasn't in our bedroom. I found her in one of the guest bedrooms, one that hadn't been used in a decade. It had a king-size bed, Italian furniture, and plenty of space for two people. She stood with her hands on her hips and surveyed the area.

I came up behind her and wrapped my arms around her waist.

She didn't flinch at my touch, like she'd been expecting me all along. Her hands glided over my arms until she reached my hands as they sat on her stomach. Her fingertips brushed against my black ring, and I could feel her metal band rub against me.

My face moved into her neck, and I kissed her, feeling her pulse right against my lips. My breath fell across her skin, entering her ear canal. "What are you doing in here?"

She turned her head and looked at me over her shoulder. "Seeing if this room is a good fit."

"A good fit for what?"

"The baby."

I hadn't thought that far into the future. She wasn't

even truly starting to show yet, so I was still just grasping the fact that there was a little person growing inside her.

"I thought we could make this into the baby's room. There's no balcony or bathroom, so there's no hazards. And it's right down the hall from our room, so I can get in here quickly if I need to."

"Excellent points."

"I thought we could repaint, set up a crib right in the middle of the room, and decorate it depending on what the gender is."

"When do we find that out?"

"Not for a few months."

"Whatever you want to do, Button. It doesn't matter to me."

"I knew you'd say that." She turned around, sliding through my arms until we were facing each other. She rose on her tiptoes and kissed me on the mouth, a subtle kiss packed with passion.

My hand slid into her hair, and I deepened the kiss, appreciating her in a way I never had before. Cane wasn't the same man he used to be after he lost the woman he loved. Button and I could have easily had a different destiny. If we both hadn't been at the right place at the right time, our paths might never have crossed. I wouldn't love someone more than anything else in this world, and I wouldn't be starting a family. Everything worked out for me. I wished it had worked out for Cane.

When Pearl pulled away, she ran her hands up my chest. "We've never had sex on this bed…"

"We haven't had sex on a lot of these beds."

"Well, you wanna start?" she asked, giving me a playful smile.

"You want to defile every bedroom in this house?"

"Why not?"

I grinned. "Even Lars's bed?"

"Ew, no," she said with a laugh. "Just the unclaimed ones."

"Alright." I lifted her up and carried her to the bed. "Let's start now."

———

A MONTH CAME AND WENT.

Button's belly started to show. Now it was slightly distended and round, pressing through her shirt to give her a noticeable mound. I'd never been into pregnant women, but once she started to show, I found it distinctly arousing.

But it was probably because she was my wife—and that was my baby.

I lay beside her in bed and rubbed her bare stomach. My hand traveled down her chest and tilted once I reached the part of her tummy that curved outward. I moved up, feeling the soft skin as it swelled with the life growing inside her. I moved to the center of her stomach and pressed my hand against it. There was no movement or sign of life, but I knew there was something beautiful in there.

Something we made together.

She rested her hand on mine. "I don't think we'll feel anything for a while."

"I wonder how big they are."

"Probably the size of my finger."

I sat up and kissed her stomach, lavishing the area with kisses. Now that I saw signs of the baby, it made me realize it was really happening. We had a son or daughter on the way. That made me excited and scared at the same time. "It's strange..."

"What?" she asked.

"How much I love this baby when I've never met them." I pressed my ear to her stomach and wondered if I would hear something. It was quiet inside, nothing but her pulse and the rumbling of her stomach.

Her eyes softened as she ran her fingers through my hair. "You're going to be a great father, Crow."

"I don't know. I'll do my best."

"You never thought you would be a great husband, but you're the best in the world."

My eyes left her gaze, and I looked at her stomach again, thinking of the way I'd slapped her after she returned from seeing Tristan. I was brutal and cold, losing my temper and doing something horrifying. It was one of my biggest regrets.

"What?" She picked up on my sudden shift in mood.

My hand moved across her stomach, and I stared at her belly button. "Nothing."

"Crow," she pressed, looking at me with those demanding eyes.

"I guess I don't agree with your statement."

"Why?"

"I just don't."

"Well, you're wrong, Crow. There's no safer place in the world than by your side."

I appreciated her love for me, her acceptance and patience. I wasn't the same man I used to be, and while I'd grown and become a better man, I still had things to change. All I could do was learn from my mistakes and improve. My weapons business was gone, and now I was a clean man. I had a chance to start over, to be the person I wanted to be. I didn't have to be the cold and brooding man I'd always been. I could be something much better.

There was a knock on the door.

It was nine in the evening, the time when Button and I retired to bed, made love, and went to sleep. Lars didn't disturb us after eight unless it was an emergency.

And that knock told me this was an emergency.

"Your Grace?" Lars said through the closed door. "I need to speak with you."

Pearl wore a worried expression as she looked at me.

I got out of bed, pulled on sweatpants and a t-shirt, and walked out. I shut the door behind me since Button was still naked in bed. "What is it?"

Lars stepped back, still wearing his tuxedo despite the late hour. "I have the police on the phone. They tried calling your cell, but I guess it's off. They called the house phone."

I usually turned off my phone at night because I didn't want to be bothered. I didn't have a criminal business anymore, so I wasn't on call during the late hours of the night. "The police? Why?"

"Apparently, Cane was arrested for drinking and driving."

I stared at my butler with the same expression on my face. I was in disbelief, but I didn't let the surprise creep into my face. I was too stunned to even react.

"They aren't going to press charges, but they want you to go down there and pick him up. They're willing to look the other way on the matter since you and Cane have always gone out of your way to ensure their safety over the years."

Cane and I never hurt a police officer, and neither did our men. Lots of criminal things had gone down during the years, and anytime the police were in a place they shouldn't be, we directed them away from the warfare. The kind of heists we were performing exceeded their abilities, and the last thing we wanted was good officers to be hurt because of our actions. They were better suited for homicides and petty crime, not drug lords and weapons kingpins. "Fuck."

"I would go in your stead, but they specifically asked for you."

"I'll handle it. Thank you, Lars."

"Of course, sir." He nodded then walked away.

I walked back into the room and pulled on my jeans and a long-sleeved shirt.

"What happened?" Button sat up in bed with the sheets pulled over her chest. Her hair was a mess from the way I'd dug my hand into it, and her lips were swollen from the way I'd sucked them so aggressively just thirty minutes ago.

"Cane is down at the police station."

"What?" Button blurted. "Why?"

I pulled my jacket over my shoulders. "Drinking and driving."

Her eyes grew wider. "You've got to be kidding me."

"I wish I were. I have to go."

"Maybe I should—"

"Your ass is staying here." I walked out of the bedroom and shut the door harder than I meant to.

———

CANE HADN'T JUST BEEN DRINKING and driving.

He was totally wasted.

He sat in the cell alone with his eyes drooping. He kept sliding down across the bench before he righted himself and sat straight. The officer told me he'd vomited a few times when I was on my way over there.

The police officer stood with me in front of the bars. "We spotted him driving down a country road. He was swerving left and right constantly. It took us a while to pull him over because he didn't seem to understand we were the police. I tried to question him, but I got mostly nonsense. I never see either of you in trouble with the law, at least like this. Everything okay?"

I'd thought Cane was getting better with every passing day. But apparently, he was only getting worse. Adelina's departure was still haunting him. "He's going through a bad breakup."

"Doesn't justify that kind of behavior. He could have killed someone."

"I know…" What if Button was on the road to pick something up from the store, and she got in Cane's way? It was a possibility too difficult to imagine.

"We're going to let it go this time. But that's it."

"I understand. And thank you."

"His car has been impounded. You'll have to get it in the morning." He unlocked the cell door and pulled it open. "Cane, someone is here to take you home."

He jolted awake and opened his eyes to look at me. He stared at me blankly like he didn't recognize who I was. But a moment later, understanding came into his expression, and he knew exactly who I was. "Fuck…"

"Get up." I wasn't going to give him a hand. He'd have to walk out of there on his own.

Cane moved at a snail's pace, holding on to everything he could before he could stand on his two feet. He swayed from side to side gently, closing his eyes as he tried to concentrate. In order for him to be this drunk, he would have had to have had more liquor than I could even conceive of. We both drank around the clock, so we were used to it. So for him to get this drunk meant his blood alcohol level must be through the roof.

I signed him out, and then we walked to my car outside. I refused to help him into the passenger's side. I let him struggle, and he even hit his head on the top of the car as he slid into the seat. It took him nearly five minutes to get his safety belt on, but I didn't wait around. I drove on while he continued to figure it out.

We spent the drive in silence, and Cane floated in and out of consciousness the entire time. He didn't say a single word to me, knowing I was pissed.

We arrived at his house twenty minutes later, and I was tempted to go back home to my wife. I wanted to sleep in my bed with my woman beside me. I wanted to listen to her breathe so I would know she was okay. I wanted my baby to be beside me, to protect both of them from every bad thing in the world.

But I couldn't leave Cane alone, not when he was this drunk.

He could choke on his own vomit and die.

We got inside the house, and he didn't make it any farther than the couch. He collapsed on the cushions and pulled his knees to his chest. His eyes closed, and he immediately drifted off to sleep.

I sat in the armchair and pulled out my phone. *I'm staying here tonight.*

Button texted back. *Is he okay?*

He's fine. But he won't be when he wakes up tomorrow morning.

CANE DIDN'T WAKE up until noon the next day.

Gerald made me breakfast and coffee, and I watched TV in the living room while I waited for Cane to get up. I should have been at work taking care of business or been at home with my wife. But instead, I was stuck here making sure Cane didn't need a ride to the hospital.

When he finally woke up, he dragged his hands down his face and groaned. His fingers moved to his temples, and I knew he was fighting a migraine.

Still didn't feel bad for him.

He finally righted himself on the couch and rubbed the sleep from his eyes. It took him nearly five minutes to understand I was sitting in the armchair beside him. He obviously had no memory of the previous evening. He probably had no idea how he got home. Maybe he didn't even remember the police station. "Crow…?"

"Yes." I stared him down, disappointment burning in my eyes. "Feel like shit?"

"A bit."

"Good." I tossed a bottle of pain pills at him.

He barely caught it before he popped the lid off and dumped two pills in his mouth. He swallowed them dry even though Gerald already left a glass of water on the sofa table. Cane rubbed his temple again then leaned back against the cushions, looking exhausted even though he'd just slept twelve hours straight.

"What the fuck, Cane?" I wasn't just pissed at him for his recklessness. I was disappointed. After everything we'd been through, how could be so careless with his own life? He was about to be an uncle. He had a brother who lived right down the road. None of that meant anything to him.

"Don't be pissed at me, but…what happened last night?"

Wow. "You were arrested for driving drunk. I picked you up at the police station and brought you here."

He rubbed his jaw and groaned. "Fuck."

"I stayed here so you wouldn't choke on your own puke, but I should have been at home with my family."

He bowed his head, squinting his eyes in shame.

"What the fuck were you thinking?"

"Isn't it obvious?" he asked. "I wasn't thinking at all."

"Is that an excuse?" I asked incredulously. "You could have killed someone last night."

"I know…"

"I don't think you do, asshole. That was the dumbest thing I've ever seen you do, and I've seen you do a lot of stupid shit."

"I went out with a few guys in Florence...had too much to drink...got carried away."

"But why would you get *that* carried away?"

He stared at the floor. "You know why, Crow."

Adelina. "Just because she's gone doesn't mean you have to sabotage your own life."

"I haven't spoken to her in a month. She hasn't called. She said she missed me, and then I never heard from her..."

"Doesn't matter. Be a man and carry on."

"Would you carry on if this was Pearl?"

No. I would never get over losing her. "Not the same thing."

"It is the same thing."

"No, I would never get wasted then get behind the wheel. And I can say that with complete confidence."

He dragged his hands down his face again. "I know it was stupid."

"Fucking stupid."

"I'll never do it again."

"Better not."

"I'm surprised the police let me go."

"They said they would give us a warning. But they won't be so nice next time."

He nodded. "That was good of them."

"I don't think so. I think they should have put you in prison for a few weeks to let the message sink in."

He sighed. "Cut me some slack. I said I was sorry and I won't do it again—"

"Cut you some slack?" I was on my feet instantly, ready for a fight even though guns weren't drawn. "No, I'm not cutting you any goddamn slack. You're all the family I have left in the world, Cane. It's just you and me. We're all that's left. If I lost you…" I couldn't even finish the thought. Cane meant more to me than anyone in the family ever did. He pissed me off, drove me insane, made me want to kill him sometimes, but at the end of the day, he was my brother. I could always rely on him no matter what. I knew if something bad happened to me, he would take my place and look after Button and my baby. It was the kind of loyalty that only existed in family.

Cane looked up at me, the devastation in his eyes.

"I'm sorry you're upset about Adelina. Really, I am. I wish it had worked out. But nearly killing yourself isn't the solution. If you want to get drunk like that again, do it here. Don't ever make a mistake like that again. I mean it."

"I won't," he whispered.

"I need your word, Cane."

"You have my word…"

I walked out of the living room without looking at him again. "I don't want to see you for a week. I can't even look at you right now…"

Chapter 22

Adelina

I rented a house just a few blocks away from my parents.

My parents weren't thrilled about me leaving and tried whatever they could to get me to stay, but I needed my own space. When I told them I found a nice little house just down the street, they finally accepted the situation since I'd be so close. When they went to work in the morning, they would drive past my house every single day.

I enrolled in school for my teaching credentials, going to the same college where I got my undergraduate degree. The attention of the media had finally started to disappear now that a month had come and gone. The news cycle changed, and they were more interested in the next election.

I was finally left in peace.

But there was no denying the fact that I was one of the most famous people in the country. When I went to the grocery store, people stared. When cars passed me on the road, drivers did a double take. If I went for a walk outside my house, people snapped pictures of me on their phones.

I didn't like it.

But I kept my head down and did my best to ignore them.

My house was nice. It was small with two bedrooms, a decent size living room, and a cute kitchen. I didn't need a lot of space because it was just me. It made the rent cheaper, so that was also a perk. I used Cane's money to pay for my first semester of school as well as my rent. I wanted to get a job, but since people were still so interested in me, I thought it was too soon.

I hoped I would have a normal life eventually.

I thought about Cane every single day. He was in my thoughts first thing in the morning, in the middle of the day, and then when I went to sleep. He was usually in my dreams too, and I was surprised a lot of them were sexual in nature.

My body missed the sex.

But I missed the rest of him too.

I wondered if he was thinking about me when I was thinking about him. I wondered if he wanted to call. I wondered why I didn't call.

The last time I'd spoken to him on the phone, I slipped up and told him I missed him.

Imagine what else I would say if I spoke to him on a regular basis. It wouldn't help me move on. It wouldn't help me get back on my feet. It would just hold me back as I tried to move forward with my life.

The campus was exactly as I remembered it, but now it was totally different.

Because all the students knew exactly who I was.

Every time I wanted to talk to a guy I thought was cute, he usually steered clear of me. Making friends was a lot harder than it used to be because people treated me like some infectious disease. Group assignments were awkward. Members of the group would meet up without me and finish the project without asking for my input.

They avoided me.

I knew they didn't hate me for what happened. I knew they just didn't know how to act. They didn't know what to say since I'd been trafficked and used as a sex slave. It's not like we needed to have a discussion about it, but just having them look at me made me uncomfortable.

I was in my hometown, but it felt like a different planet.

It didn't feel right.

The only thing that hadn't changed were my parents. They treated me like I was delicate, but they were just as happy to see me as they'd always been. My mom still made dinner for me and dropped it off because she knew I wasn't much of a cook.

I missed Gerald.

I missed the smell of the Tuscan countryside, the way

the olive branches stuck out and brought shade to the back-yard. I missed the sight of the vineyards, the smell of wine. I missed sleeping in that enormous bed with supersoft sheets.

And I missed the man I spent my time with.

Would this feeling ever go away?

Or was Cane right about everything?

This place wasn't my home anymore.

He was home.

I had dinner in front of the TV that night then did some work on my computer. My teaching credential program was all about papers and group projects. In a few months, I would be placed into a classroom for my student teaching. I looked forward to that the most. That was the aspect of the job that excited me. I wanted to work with kids every day, to impact their lives the way they impacted mine.

But I had to do this first.

I finished my work then went to bed. I'd bought new furniture since my parents didn't want to part with my old things. They wanted to hold on to it because it still contained my essence. If I ever got married and moved away, they wanted me to have somewhere to stay when I visited.

I couldn't picture myself getting married.

No man even wanted to look at me.

I was damaged goods to them. I was disgusting. I was a victim.

I lay in the dark but couldn't sleep. I had class first thing in the morning, but that didn't make my eyes shut. I stared at the ceiling, wearing the shirt I'd stolen from Cane. I wondered if he'd noticed the theft over the last few weeks. Or maybe he had so many shirts he didn't even care.

I stared at my phone, and a sinking sensation started in my stomach.

I missed him.

I missed him more now than ever before.

But I shouldn't call him. I shouldn't interrupt his life. If he was moving on, I didn't want to sabotage that.

But I had no one else in the world to talk to. He was the only person who really understood me. He was the only man who knew what I'd been through. I didn't need to explain anything to him. He understood me.

My resilience waned, and I picked up the phone.

It must be early in the morning there. He was probably at work or having breakfast. Or maybe he was out on a run. I wouldn't know until he answered.

He picked up quickly, answering on the second ring. *"Bellissima."*

It was the most beautiful word I'd ever heard. It possessed a much deeper greeting than it seemed on the surface. It encompassed so much of our relationship, so much of the connection between us. "I hope this isn't a bad time."

"Day or night, it's never a bad time," he said quietly.

"What are you doing?"

"I'm sitting in my car at the vineyard. I just parked."

"How's the weather?"

"Sunny with no clouds," he said. "The sun rose a few hours ago, and the grapes are gleaming in the light. We're doing a harvest today, so we have a lot of locals coming down to help us pick the fruit."

"That sounds nice."

"Not a bad way to spend my day."

"No..." I turned on my side and closed my eyes, wishing I was standing beside him in Tuscan paradise.

"How's life in South Carolina?" He sounded the same way he did before, lighthearted and easygoing. He didn't seem sad the way he had at the airport. He was either putting on a good performance, or he'd accepted the fact that I was living a new life.

"It's okay." I wanted to tell him it was great, that I loved school and everything else about my life. I wanted to tell him I met new friends and reconnected with old ones. I wanted to say my parents and I took a family trip even though we couldn't go anywhere without being recognized. But I didn't say any of that since it wasn't true.

"Are you having a hard time?" he asked quietly.

"It's not...not what I expected."

He was silent, inviting me to continue.

"Everyone knows who I am. Everywhere I go, people take pictures of me. My story had a lot of media coverage, so all my classmates know everything that happened to me. People walk on eggshells around me like I might explode any minute. My old friends don't know how to behave around me. Not a single guy has asked me out. I haven't gotten a job because I know people will be weird when they interact with me…"

He sighed into the phone. "I'm sorry to hear that." Even though he'd warned me of this, he seemed sincere. "What about your parents?"

"They're the one thing that hasn't changed. We play board games together and still sit down for our meals. That's nice. But that's the only thing that's enjoyable."

"At least you have them."

"Yeah…I moved in to a little house down the street. I needed my own space, and they were reluctant to let me go. But now they're okay with it."

"It's in a nice area, right?" The protective side of him emerged, a version of him that would never die, no matter how many miles separated us.

"Very nice."

"Did you buy it?"

"No, just renting."

Cane didn't express his disappointment that I hadn't bought anything. "I wish things were better for you, *Bellissima*. All I can say is, it should get better in time. In a few years, people will forget about your story."

I didn't want to wait years to have a normal life. "Yeah…"

Cane sat on the phone with me in silence, enjoying my presence even when we didn't have a conversation.

"Last time we were on the phone, you told me you missed me."

I held my breath.

"You hung up on me before I could say it back. So I'm going to say it now. I miss you too, *Bellissima*."

I closed my eyes and felt my chest ache.

"Your clothes are still in the closet. Your makeup is still in my bathroom. I still don't sleep on your side of the bed because I'm so used to having you there. It's a habit I can't break."

I didn't have a response to such beautiful words, so I didn't say anything at all. Tears were already in my eyes, and I wished I were sitting beside him in that car. I wished I could look at his face, touch his beard.

When Cane knew I wasn't going to say anything, he changed the subject. "Pearl is starting to show. I can see her belly through her shirts."

"Aww…"

"Crow is really happy. I can tell he's taken to fatherhood pretty well, even though the baby isn't here yet."

"He'll be a great dad."

"Yeah, he will be," he whispered. "Other than that, there's been nothing new going on. We're still working on the second winery, and I've taken over at the original one so Crow can be home with Pearl more."

"That's nice."

The silence returned to the conversation. We sat together and absorbed the unspoken tension between us. I knew Cane didn't want to get off the phone even though he had nothing to say, and I didn't want to get off the phone either. I wanted him beside me right then and there.

But I couldn't tell him that.

After another five minutes of silence, Cane spoke. "I should get to work…"

"Yeah, I should get some sleep."

"You can call me for anything, *Bellissima*. Even if you just want someone to talk to."

"I know."

"Good night."

"Good night." I wanted to hear him say he loved me even if I didn't say it back. I wanted to feel his love wrap around me, to make me feel safe in this foreign land. I felt like I was on a different planet, walking the surface with aliens rather than people.

"I love you." He hung up immediately, cutting the line before I had the chance to say anything back—or to say nothing back.

And I knew that was why he did it.

Chapter 23

CANE

After my drinking incident, I steered clear of booze.

It was too soon to trust myself around it.

When I went out with those guys in Florence, I'd just wanted a distraction so I would stop thinking about Adelina. If a woman flirted with me and wanted sex, I was going to do it so I could drown my sorrow in someone else.

But when the women came up to me, I didn't take the bait.

I didn't want them.

Women used to cure my other sicknesses, but now it wasn't effective. So I turned to alcohol instead and drank way too much. I got so drunk that I still don't remember most of that night. I didn't even remember getting behind the wheel to drive home. I didn't remember getting pulled over. I didn't remember my brother taking me home.

It was pathetic.

I didn't see Crow for a week because I knew he wasn't joking.

He didn't want to look at my face.

I completely understood. I didn't want to look at my face much either.

When I walked into the winery that day, I felt weak and hopeless. I'd just spoken to Adelina, but that didn't uplift me. It hurt that she was unhappy. It hurt me that people treated her like a victim rather than the badass woman she was. It bothered me that she didn't feel like she belonged there anymore.

I'd be lying if I said I didn't want her to give up and come back.

But I also wanted her to be happy.

It was the first unselfish moment I'd ever had, and that made me feel worse. It made me realize I truly loved this woman from the bottom of my heart. My love for her was selfless, real, and deep. I treated her the way Crow treated Pearl—like she was the only thing that mattered.

The realization created a powerful wave of sadness.

I walked into the warehouse and struggled to focus on what I was supposed to do. My mind kept flicking back to Adelina, imagining her lying in her bed all alone. She was doing that right now, probably still thinking about me.

I told her I loved her and didn't care if she wouldn't say it back.

I wanted her to know I still loved her just as much—even if the rest of the world just saw her as entertainment.

Crow walked inside a few minutes later, wearing a black suit. The atmosphere around his body was still slightly hostile, and I knew it would be that way for a while until he truly forgave me for what I did.

Right now, I didn't really care.

Crow talked about the shipments going out that afternoon, giving me a refresher even though I hadn't forgotten anything. It'd only been a week. All I'd been doing during that time was thinking about Adelina and the fact that I wasn't working because my brother didn't want to see my face.

I nodded along without really caring.

Crow eyed me suspiciously, knowing my mind was elsewhere. "What's up?"

"Adelina just called me when I pulled up." I grabbed the shipping information from the clipboard then checked the serial numbers against the barrels.

"She did?" Crow came to my side and grabbed the clipboard from my hand. "What did she say?"

"It's been hard for her to adjust. People see her as entertainment."

"Because her story was all over the news?"

I nodded. "She's not loving it. Feels a little lost."

"Did she say she wants to come back?" he asked.

"No…" I'd been hoping to hear that, but it never came.

I wasn't going to push her in any direction. If she wanted to come back, she had to make that decision on her own.

"But she hates it there?"

"She didn't say she hated it. She just doesn't love it."

Crow set the clipboard off to the side. "You need to go get her, Cane."

"What?"

"Go get her," he repeated. "You let her go because that's what she wanted. But now she told you it's not working out like she thought. That means you need to go there and remind why she needs to come back. That's your woman—so go get her."

"That's the exact opposite of what you told me to do in the first place."

"It's not," he said. "She wanted to leave, and you had to let her go. Holding her hostage wasn't the answer. But now, she's lost. Now, she's unhappy. She's living in a world where people make her feel like she's dirty. Go talk to her."

There was nothing I wanted more. I was only partially living in this miserable existence. Time passed slowly because my life had no meaning. I was heartbroken, but it was a kind of broken that couldn't be fixed.

"I'm serious," Crow said. "Go."

"That's what you would do if this were Pearl?"

He shook his head. "I'd be halfway to the airport right now."

I HOPPED on the plane and landed in America an eternity later. Due to the time change, connections, and the long flights, it was nighttime there. I wanted to rush to her house and knock on her front door, but it was too late for that.

I'd have to wait until tomorrow.

I checked into the same hotel I stayed at with her the last time I was there.

Crow called me after I'd been there for an hour. "Hey, you're on the ground, right?"

"You sound worried," I teased.

"Just want to make sure. Your flight info isn't popping up on the website."

It seemed like he wasn't mad at me anymore. "Did you get that information for me?"

"Yeah. I got her address. Wasn't hard to find. Are you going now?"

"No. It's almost eleven here. She might be asleep already."

"You have the patience to wait until tomorrow?" he asked incredulously.

"I want to do this right."

"And what exactly are you going to do?" he asked.

"I'll swing by and ask her to dinner."

"Not a bad idea."

"I want to show her that I couldn't care less about what she went through. While everyone else stares at her like some kind of freak, I see her as the beautiful woman she really is. I want her in my bed for the rest of my life. I'm man enough to erase every memory she has of the others. It'll be like they were never there at all."

Crow paused over the line. "You should tell her that."

"I will."

"Let me know how it goes. Pearl and I both hope she comes back with you."

"That makes three of us."

———

I WAITED until the evening before I pulled up to the front of her house. It was a petite little place, positioned between two bigger houses. It was much smaller than the mansion she shared with me, but it somehow reminded me of her.

It fit her perfectly.

The sun had just set, and the night deepened. I stared at the front door for a moment and studied the windows. I noticed the gentle blue light that was shifting, obviously the light projected from a TV screen.

She was home.

I got out of the car and walked up the sidewalk until I reached her front porch. I hadn't seen her in six weeks. She might look different. Her hair could be longer. She could be thinner or heavier. She could look sad or happy. I really didn't know what to expect.

I stood there as I tried to gather my thoughts. She would be shocked to see me on the other side of her door. I just hoped happiness would linger behind once the surprise faded away. My knuckles rested against the wood, and I took a long pause before I finally knocked.

It was happening.

There was no going back now.

I heard her footsteps from inside the house. She came closer and closer until she stopped right in the entryway.

I knew she was looking through the peephole first.

Good girl.

I wondered what her expression was once she realized it was me. Her eyes probably snapped wide open, and her lips parted with the deep breath she took. Her heart was slamming against her ribs as it raced.

The lock clicked, and she opened the door.

When I got a glimpse of her, I lost my breath. She was as beautiful as I remembered, with long brown hair and mocha eyes. She wore a long-sleeved shirt and black jeans with bare feet. She was over a foot shorter than me, but she made up for her petiteness with her presence. She was curvy, sexy, and absolutely perfect.

I missed her more now than I had before.

She held on to the door for balance as she processed what she was witnessing. Her eyes shifted back and forth as she looked into my expression, seeing the man she would recognize anywhere. She could pick out my voice in a crowded room with a blindfold over her eyes. She opened her mouth to say something, but nothing came out.

"Want to have dinner with me?" I had a speech prepared about being in town on business, but I thought it was a pointless thing to say. She would see right through that. The obvious reason I was there was just to see her.

She let go of the door as a smile replaced her surprise.

Exactly as I hoped.

"Yes…I'd love to."

———

I TOOK her by the hand and guided her to the table the hostess was leading us to. We took our seats, got our menus, and then we were alone together again.

It was the first time we'd eaten together in public.

It was basically our first date—our first real date.

She held her menu open between her hands, but she kept sneaking glances at me.

I didn't look at my menu at all, far more interested in looking at her. She didn't look different at all. Not a single thing had changed. I expected to spot the melancholy in her eyes, but that didn't exist. Perhaps when she was with me, she actually felt some form of happiness.

At least I hoped.

She looked down at her menu again, a smile on her lips.

I missed that smile. "You're just as beautiful as I remember."

A blush filled her cheeks. "Thanks…"

I glanced at my menu, picked something decent, and set my menu aside. I rested my elbows on the table and leaned close to her, wanting there to be as little distance as possible.

She closed her menu and set it to the side.

"What are you having?"

"Some pasta. I just picked something."

"Me too." I felt the corners of my lips pull into a smile.

The waiter came over, and judging by the way he stared at Adelina so intently, he recognized her. "Uh, what can I get for you?"

We ordered and handed our menus over.

The waiter stared again, his eyes narrowing as he remembered exactly where he'd seen her face before.

"Is there a problem?" I kept my voice low, but my coldness was unmistakable.

"No...not at all." He walked away, leaving us alone again.

Adelina dropped her smile at the encounter.

I reached my hand across the table, and I held hers. I should keep my affection to a minimum, but I couldn't. Now that I had her so close, I couldn't restrain myself. I missed her like crazy. I missed her even more now that I was directly across from her.

Her hand latched on to mine immediately, like she'd been hoping for the affection.

We ignored the basket of bread on the table and stared at each other. Just like the silent conversations we had over the phone, we were doing the same now. It was full of the same intensity, the same longing.

She never asked why I was there.

I didn't feel the need to explain.

We just savored each other's company in the crowded room, ignoring the inappropriate stares directed our way. People were casting judgments on both of us. She was holding hands with a man at least five years older than her. She was already seeing someone after what she'd been through? I wanted to be with a woman that had been trafficked? A million thoughts were going through their minds.

But they didn't know us. No one did.

The only two people who truly understood were she and I.

———

WE WALKED into her little house, and she showed me the living room and small kitchen. "It's not much, but it's perfect for me."

"I like it." It had a single sofa, a small TV, and a tiny bathroom. For a woman like Adelina, someone who didn't need much, it was perfect. "Very nice." I stood with my hands in my pockets so I wouldn't immediately reach out and grab her by the hips. So far, it seemed to be going well. She smiled when she looked at me, held my hand on the car ride home, and now she gave me the same look of longing I gave her.

Just like in the restaurant, it was tense all over again.

She still hadn't asked me why I was there. It made me wonder if she didn't care. Maybe she was just so happy to see me that it didn't matter.

I stepped closer to her until I'd officially crossed an invisible line into her private space. My hands left my pockets, and my neck craned toward her. I looked down at her lips, desperate to kiss her.

Her lips parted slightly.

That was the invitation I needed. My hand slid into her hair, and I leaned in, moving until I felt her lips against mine. I kissed her with purposeful slowness, doing my best to keep it soft. I couldn't devour her immediately. This had to be gentle, not rushed.

She kissed me back immediately, her arm wrapped around my neck. She rose on her tiptoes to get better access to my mouth. She kissed me harder, a moan of desperation escaping her lips. Her hand wrapped around my wrist as my hand remained buried in her hair.

She was the one who kissed me harder.

Deeper.

Faster.

I couldn't set the pace anymore. I wanted to keep it slow and soft, but she wanted a lot more than that. So I let it be...and kissed her exactly the way she wanted to be kissed.

My hands explored her body, feeling the delicious curves of her waist and stomach. My hands shook as I felt her, excitement burning me from the inside out. My desperation grew, and I couldn't believe what was happening.

I was kissing her.

Just last week, I was drowning myself in enough alcohol to put me in a coma.

But now, my woman was in my arms.

She pulled on the front of my shirt and guided me down the short hallway to her bedroom. She had a full-size bed in the small room, a mattress hardly big enough to hold a man like me. But that wasn't going to stop either of us from getting what we wanted.

Her shirt was gone.

My shoes were kicked across the room.

Her bra dropped onto the floor.

My jeans were yanked down.

One by one, every article of clothing hit the carpet until we were both buck naked.

I squeezed her tits and kissed her neck, her smell making me high. I kissed her hard, nibbled on her earlobe, and guided her back to the bed. My cock was harder than it'd ever been in my life. I'd never seen a woman look so beautiful, so undeniably perfect.

She was on her back underneath me, her legs already spread in urgency. She pulled me on top of her and hooked her arms around my shoulders.

I slipped inside, moaning when I felt how soaked she was. She was wetter than she'd ever been before, tight and slick. I pushed completely inside her and watched her face light up in pleasure.

She wanted me badly.

One hand dug into my hair, and she stared up at me as I began to thrust. I thought we would take this slow, but she didn't want slow. She wanted all of me, as much as she could get. She pulled on my hair and kissed me, moaning between breaths. "Cane…"

"*Bellissima…*" There was nothing better than this. There was nothing that would ever make me as happy as this woman. I'd lost her before, and it was a depressing experience. Now that I was with her again, even without saying much, I felt whole again.

This felt right.

It always felt right.

I hadn't been with anyone else in the last six weeks, so I thought I would come quicker than I wanted. But being connected to her like this stopped that from happening. I focused on her, focused on the way she moved her lips with mine. My cock was buried inside her, but the satisfaction I received was beyond physical.

It was spiritual.

She moved with me, taking my length as much as I gave it to her. Sweat collected on her breasts, and she moaned into my mouth as we made love on her small bed. She dug her nails into my back, and she pulled me deeper and harder.

Sweat trickled down my back, but the heat didn't slow me down. I wanted to do this forever. If I could, I would.

She cupped the back of my neck with both of her hands and used her abs to grind with me. "Cane…I love you." She looked me in the eye as she said it, the passion in her eyes and the promise on her face.

I shoved myself completely inside her and paused as I

stared down at her. I'd told her how I felt many times, but she never said it back. All I could do was imagine how it would feel, but reality was so much better than fantasy. It was the most beautiful thing I'd ever heard. It made me the happiest man on the planet. "I love you too."

———

I WOKE up to her body plastered against mine. One leg was hooked between my thighs, while her arm draped across my torso. She used my shoulder as a pillow for her head, and she slept nearly on top of me. It was the same position she used to take before, and the second I was with her again, she was back to her old ways.

Instead of stirring, I remained absolutely still so I could watch her. I loved her thick eyelashes. I loved the way her lips slightly parted while she was asleep. Her fair skin contrasted against those ruby lips even when she didn't wear lipstick. She was right beside me, but I could hardly believe she was real.

She was perfect.

I wanted to lean down and kiss her, but she was too beautiful to interrupt. I wanted her to be wide awake so I could look into those pretty eyes, but I wanted her to rest as long as she needed. When I came to her doorstep, I hadn't expected for this to happen.

But I'd hoped it would.

She'd said the most beautiful words to me. The world

outside hadn't changed, but mine certainly did. Now this cold and dark place blossomed with extraordinary beauty. My body was filled with unrestrained vitality. My attitude was positive, my smile was infectious.

I was happy.

A few minutes later, her eyes fluttered open. She looked right at me, the same smile coming over her lips. "Just like it used to be…"

I usually woke up first, and I spent my morning staring at her until she was ready to wake up. My body wanted to roll her to her back and thrust between her legs, but my heart was content just being like this. "But better."

She ran her hand up my chest, her eyes still sleepy. She released a sigh of contentment, enjoying my presence as much as I enjoyed hers.

I was so glad I got on that plane.

"I forgot to thank you for dinner."

"You showed your appreciation, *Bellissima*." My hand brought hers to my mouth. I kissed her small fingers gently before I returned them to my chest.

"Sex gets me food?" she teased.

"It can get you whatever you want."

Her alarm went off on her nightstand, and she sighed before she turned over and switched it off. Her bare back was exposed, smooth skin with the exception of a few scars. "I have class."

I forgot about the real world whenever we were together. "Are you going to go?"

She shook her head before she came back to me. "I doubt I'll ever get out of this bed."

"Because I'm in it?" I moved underneath the sheets until I was on top of her. My legs parted hers until I was nestled perfectly between her thighs. My hands sank into the mattress on either side of her tits. With a quick tilt of my hips, I pressed my cock against her entrance.

Her arms circled my neck, and she locked her ankles against my lower back. "I miss morning sex…"

I slid the rest of the way inside her until I was buried to the hilt. I closed my eyes as I treasured the feel of her wet tightness. I used to do this every single day of my life. I'd never take it for granted again. There was nowhere I'd rather be than right here. "I miss this pussy."

"She missed you too."

I thrust into her gradually, making love a lot slower than we did last night. My eyes were locked on hers, and she looked stunning in the morning light. Her skin was glowing from a great night of sleep, and her eyes sparkled in a special way. Her nails teased me gently as her feet dragged me back toward her. *"Bellissima…"*

"I miss hearing you call me that."

I sealed my mouth over hers and kissed her as I continued to rock deeply inside her. I pushed myself as far as I could go without hurting her then pulled out again. Her mattress was soft like a cloud, and her pussy was like a slice of heaven.

I couldn't think straight. All I could do was feel—feel all of her.

She came quicker than usual, squeezing my dick and digging her nails into my muscles.

I wanted to keep going, but after her little performance, I wouldn't be able to sustain this passion without needing a release. I came shortly after she did, filling her pussy with all of the seed I could fit inside.

I stayed on top of her because I didn't want to leave. I wanted to stay right there, between her legs where I belonged. No amount of hunger could get me into the kitchen. I'd rather just eat her.

The sleepiness was gone from her eyes. A small smile was on her lips, just for me.

We still hadn't said anything of substance to one another. The second I was back in her life, it was exactly what it used to be before. The house wasn't the same, the town was foreign, and her world was nothing like mine.

But that didn't change us.

Her nails dragged down my arms as her hands moved to the mattress. "Why are you here?"

My hand slid into her hair, and I cradled her head in my palm. "You know why."

Her eyes softened. "I tried not to think about you...but it was impossible."

"I never stopped thinking about you. Every day."

She brushed her nose against mine. "Your bed hasn't been filled with others?"

"Just you."

Her eyes softened again.

I didn't ask her the same because I already knew the answer. "We can spend the rest of the day like this, but let's leave in the morning. I want to get you home where you belong."

It was the first time she'd shown sadness since I arrived. Her eyes fell, and her smile disappeared. "Leave?"

I'd assumed that's what would happen. "Are you saying you want to stay?" I'd do anything for this woman, but I didn't belong in a place like this. The population was too dense. There wasn't enough privacy. I had a business back home. There was nothing for me—except her.

"I just…I can't leave."

"Why not?"

"My parents. After everything they've been through, I can't just take off again. They're so happy having me here. It's like a massive boulder has been lifted off their shoulders. I can't hurt them again… I can't."

"They know you'll be safe, so it'll be different."

"I'll be in a different time zone on the other side of the world. I'll never see them. After I was captured, it made me appreciate what I have. I don't want to take them for granted again. I don't want them to suffer again."

She was the only child of these two people. She'd already suffered enough, and she shouldn't suffer anymore. But I didn't know how to fix the problem. "I can't stay here, even for you." My eyes held their determination despite my sorrow. "I don't belong here. There's nothing for me to do here. It makes more sense for you to come back with me. We have the winery, a beautiful home overlooking the fields, and we have millions. I can't just bring that money here. Your country has very different laws from mine."

"I know…"

"So we need to make it work, *Bellissima*. I've spent the last six weeks without you, and I don't want to do it anymore. You're coming back with me—even if I have to make you."

She smiled because she thought I was joking. "Back to being bossy, huh?"

"I'm just telling you how it is." Now that she told me she loved me, there was no going back. She was my possession, my everything. I owned her, even if the law didn't recognize it. If she had any hope of slipping out of my grasp, she shouldn't have said those three little words.

"I don't know what to do, Cane. I've only been back for a few weeks."

"Your parents will understand. Children get married and move away all the time."

"It's different, and you know it is."

I did know. I sighed as my softening cock remained buried inside her. When the mood picked up, I'd be ready to go again.

She stared at me with a pleading gaze, as if she was asking me to help her.

"What do you want me to say?" I whispered.

"I don't know…"

"I can't move here." I repeated it because I knew she would ask me. "I have Crow, Pearl, and my future niece or nephew. Crow won't admit it, but he needs me nearby. I'm all he has left, and he's all I have left. You know I would do anything for you, *Bellissima*, but I can't do that."

When she released a deep breath, all of her hope vanished with it. "I understand."

Even now, I wanted to give her what she wanted. But this was one compromise I couldn't make. "Let's talk to your parents. I'm sure they'll understand when they see us together."

"I don't know…"

"What other choice do we have?" I wasn't returning to Tuscany without her, and she couldn't continue this lonely existence in a world where she no longer belonged. "This isn't your home anymore. You tried, but it wouldn't stick. You know you belong with me in the Tuscan sun and in the fields of gold."

Her eyes shifted back and forth as she looked into my gaze. She pressed her lips tightly together, thought it through, and then finally nodded. "Okay…let's talk to them."

I TURNED OFF THE ENGINE, and we sat in front of her parents' house. It was after five, so they were both home from work. I stayed behind the wheel while she looked out the window of the passenger seat. We'd spent the afternoon making love all over her small house. Her shower was tiny, but we somehow made it work. We didn't eat much because we were too absorbed in each other.

Now those moments of happiness were gone. Dread had replaced them. Adelina didn't want to do this, but she didn't have any other option.

"We can always visit them whenever you want," I whispered. "It's not like it's forever. I see Crow and Pearl every day. We can spend every holiday with your family. That's a fair compromise."

"I know…but we're so close."

My hand glided up her shoulder, and I massaged her gently. "It'll be alright, *Bellissima*." Her mother had thanked me for getting Adelina back home, but that didn't necessarily mean they liked me. She was my prisoner at one point. I did business with the man who hurt her. I wasn't the knight in shining armor they'd been hoping for for their daughter. I was dark, brooding, and dangerous.

After a few more minutes of waiting, Adelina finally got out.

We walked to the front door, knocked, and then we were face-to-face with her parents.

They both recognized me. They definitely remembered me.

Her mother stared at me, not smiling or frowning. She just looked.

Her father didn't know how to react either.

"Can we come in?" Adelina asked.

"Of course." Her mother backed inside, still looking at me. "I'm sorry…you just startled us."

We stepped into the living room, the smell of dinner in the air.

"Everything okay?" her father asked.

"Yeah," Adelina said, hardly convincing. "If you guys aren't busy, we wanted to talk to you about something."

"Sure," her mother said. "Would you like to join us for dinner?"

"Yeah," Adelina said.

I hadn't said anything up until that point, and I knew I needed to show some manners. "We'd love to."

We sat down in the dining room, and her mom served baked chicken, green beans, and potatoes.

I didn't have much of an appetite, but I ate anyway. It was pretty good.

Adelina ate and talked to her parents about school, even though that wasn't why we were there.

"So, are you here for a visit?" her mother asked.

I swallowed my tap water before I turned to her. "I just wanted to make sure Adelina was doing alright…adjusting back to her old life."

"Oh," her mother said. "That was nice of you."

"She's gotten back on her feet," her father said. "Has her own place now and is back in school." The pride was heavy in his voice, as it should be. Adelina was a strong woman who didn't let the past define her. She never gave up on herself—not once.

"I noticed that," I said. "I'm happy for her."

Adelina looked up at me, the sadness in her eyes. She didn't want to say the words, to break their hearts with her news.

My hand moved to her thigh under the table, and I gave it a gentle squeeze, telling her I would take care of it. "I came back here because I wanted to know Adelina was doing okay…but also because I love her."

Her mother didn't react in the slightest, as if she already expected my feelings.

Her father looked down at his food.

"I stayed away from her because she said she wanted to come back here and start over…but she told me she's been having a hard time. She misses me, I miss her…and she loves me." I watched Adelina's emotional expression, waiting for the final blow. "We talked about it, and we decided that we want to be together…in Italy."

Her mother dropped her silverware onto the plate, unable to contain her surprise.

Her father looked up, tensing all over his body. Even his jaw was hard.

Tears immediately welled up in her mother's eyes. "Adelina, is this true?"

Adelina finally looked at her mother. "Yes…I want to be with him. I know he and I didn't meet under the best of circumstances, but…I don't want to be with anyone else.

He's the only one who really understands me. Everyone else looks at me like I'm a freak, but Cane never does. He makes me feel beautiful when the rest of the world makes me feel scared. I've tried moving on, but this place doesn't feel the way it used to…"

"I see," her father whispered.

Her mother dabbed her eyes with a napkin.

I felt like shit watching this scene, so I could only imagine how Adelina felt.

"I'm sorry," Adelina whispered. "I don't want to leave you guys again, but I can't stay. Cane has his business and properties in Tuscany. He can't just walk away from that."

Her mother started to cry. "We just got you back…"

"I know, Mama." Now Adelina started to cry.

Even her father was choked up.

I didn't want to rip apart a family. I wanted Adelina so much, but I didn't want to cause her pain. Her parents had been nice to me even when I didn't deserve it, and I didn't want to do this to them. "I have another idea."

Adelina wiped the corner of her eye with her fingers. "What?"

Her mother's eyes were puffy and red. She had the same eyes as Adelina, and she possessed the same beauty Adelina had inherited.

I grabbed Adelina's hand under the table. "Come with us."

"What?" her father blurted.

"We have jobs and a mortgage," her mother said. "We

can't just drop everything for a vacation."

"I'll take care of everything," I said. "I'll buy you a house and some land nearby. You can see Adelina every day while I'm at work."

Adelina gave me the biggest look of surprise I'd ever seen. Her mouth was open, and her eyes were filled with shock. "Really?"

"Are you being serious?" her mother asked. "You would do that?"

Adelina kept staring at me. "Cane? Are you sure about this?"

I squeezed her hand. "I've never been more sure of anything in my life." If I was going to take Adelina back with me, she was bound to become my wife. And if I had a wife, I knew I would do anything in my power to give her whatever she wanted. If she needed her parents, I would give that to her. It was a small investment to make this woman happy.

Adelina's eyes filled with tears but for a different reason than before. "I love you."

I smiled at the affection in her eyes. "I know you do, *Bellissima*."

"You would do that for us?" her mother pressed. "That's very generous…"

"Extremely generous," her father said.

"Does that mean you're saying yes?" I asked. "It would solve all of our problems. And trust me, you're going to love Tuscany. I've never seen a more beautiful place."

"Uh…" Her mother stared at her father, the disbelief on her face.

He stared back, rubbing the side of his face.

"This is the only way I can keep all of us together," I said. "I'll buy you a beautiful home with plenty of privacy. You'll never have to worry about anything. If you say no, then we're going to live on opposites sides of the world for the rest of our lives."

Adelina turned back to her parents, waiting for the answer she was hoping for.

Her mother and father whispered to each other on their side of the table, keeping their voices low so we couldn't overhear. After a few minutes, they turned back to us.

Her mother gave us the answer. "We'd love to."

Adelina exploded out of her chair and moved into my lap. She sat right down on me and wrapped her arms around my neck, hugging me hard like no one else was in the room. "Thank you…"

I squeezed her back and rested my chin on the top of her head. "I'd do anything for you."

"I'm sorry I stayed away for so long… I'm sorry I didn't tell you I loved you."

"It's okay, *Bellissima*." It had hurt feeling her rejection, but now that I had her, it didn't matter anymore. Now, we were together, and nothing would keep us apart. "Forget about it."

"I don't doubt you love my daughter," her mother said. "But I hope we aren't changing all of our lives for something that isn't concrete." Her meaning was unmistakable, probably because she intended it that way.

I wasn't bringing Adelina all the way across the world so she could be my prisoner again. I wanted her to be something more important than that. If she hadn't left, I would have asked her already. I didn't have a ring, but my intent had been living in my heart for a long time. "*Bellissima*, will you marry me?"

Adelina gripped my arm for balance and lost her breath. As if she couldn't believe what she'd heard, she stared at my expression for confirmation.

"I didn't mean right this second," her mother said. "I just meant…"

"I don't have a ring," I whispered. "But I'll get you whatever ring you want. I don't want a big wedding because I don't have a big family or many friends. But I want to spend the rest of my life with you. I never want to be apart from you again, and I promise I'll always take care of you. You'll never have to worry about anything as long as you live."

"Cane…" Her hand cupped my cheek, and tears streamed down her face. "Yes."

I smiled, seeing this woman love me as much as I loved her. I should have known how she felt when I dropped her off at the airport. I should have known she was trying to fight the same feelings I had embraced.

"Yes," she repeated. "Now take me home."

Chapter 24

ADELINA

My dress was too tight, but I refused to loosen it.

I'd suck in my stomach the entire time if I had to.

I wore a simple dress, off-white with a subtle design of beads in the front. My hair was pulled back with a single pink flower tucked behind my ear. My mother gave me her bracelet to wear, and Pearl gave me one of her necklaces.

I looked at myself in the mirror and felt the nervousness in my stomach.

I wasn't nervous about the man I was going to marry.

I was nervous to get down the stairs without him to hold me.

We were having a simple ceremony in the backyard. My parents had a house down the road, which they both loved. Everyone had settled in quickly, and the second I was back in Tuscany, I felt right at home.

South Carolina felt like a foreign country to me.

Tuscany was my home now. Cane was my home.

I was about to become a Barsetti, a name that rolled off the tongue so easily. I would gain a brother and a sister, and my family would grow. My parents accepted Cane and knew he was a good man, despite the way our story began. He took care of me, provided for them, and showed his astounding commitment to me. They couldn't ask for more.

Pearl walked through the door. "Are you ready?"

"Yeah, I think so." I turned away from the mirror and looked at her, seeing the large bump of her stomach.

"Good. Because Cane is starting to get moody."

"I'm not late," I argued.

"Yeah, but he's in a bit of a hurry."

"Why?"

She smiled. "The sooner you're officially his, the happier he'll be. That's my guess…based on being married to his brother."

A smile stretched across my lips because I knew she was right. I walked to the window and peeked into the backyard. Cane stood there in a black suit and tie, his hair styled. He looked handsome and hard under the afternoon sunlight. He'd shaved his face so his chin was clean and smooth. He looked across the fields, probably thinking of a million things at once.

Crow came to his side and placed his arm around his shoulders. They spoke to each other in private, a few smiles exchanged.

Pearl came to my side. "They act like tough shit all the time, but they're just a bunch of girls."

I smiled. "They are."

"I'd never thought in a million years I would have married someone like Crow. If you'd told me that before I was captured, I wouldn't have believed it. It went against everything I stood for. But now…there's nowhere else in the world I belong. I'm sure you feel the same way about Cane. He's not what you expected. He's not even what you wanted. But he's exactly what you need…"

My eyes were still on Cane. "You described it perfectly."

———

IT WASN'T my dream wedding.

But it was perfect for us.

My father escorted me down the aisle until I reached Cane under my favorite oak tree. He didn't wear a smile of joy like most grooms, but he stared at me with intense possession. He wanted to snatch me away from my father the second I was within range. He wanted to make me his forever, to make me a Barsetti. He wanted that name to be on my tombstone and last for the rest of time.

When my father released me, Cane didn't hesitate before he grabbed my hand and pulled me into his side. Once his hands were on me, the intensity in his gaze relaxed. He pulled me close to him and kissed me on the cheek, his touch delicate.

Crow stood beside him, and he smiled at his brother.

Cane turned me to the priest, his hand held tightly in mine. The vows were read, but Cane seemed only to be repeating them. He stared at me with a different message in his eyes, telling me he loved me because of everything we'd endured. He saw me as a strong woman who never gave up. He saw me as the perfect partner to share his life with. He saw me as the one treasure he would guard forever.

I hardly listened to the priest myself.

Despite the fact that so much had changed, this felt right. I didn't belong in America anymore. I belonged in the vineyards under the sun. I belonged in that big bed with this huge man beside me. I was meant to be a Barsetti and nothing else.

I never believed in destiny or fate, but now, I wasn't so sure.

Maybe those terrible things were meant to happen to me. Maybe they were meant to strengthen me, to make me resilient despite the pain. Maybe they were meant to bring me across the ocean to find the one man who was perfect for me.

Maybe this was all preordained.

"Do you take this woman to be your lawfully wedded wife?" the priest asked.

Cane squeezed both of my hands and moved closer to me, ready to kiss me even though it wasn't time. "I do."

"And do you take this man to be your lawfully wedded husband?" the priest asked.

"I do——"

Cane's hands were on my face, and his lips were on my mouth. He kissed me before the words were fully out of my mouth. He couldn't wait to love me, to make me officially his. A real man loved his woman with everything he had, and there was no doubt Cane loved me with all his heart.

Crow snickered then clapped, getting everyone else to clap along with him.

"Uh…kiss the bride," the priest said awkwardly.

My hands moved to Cane's powerful shoulders, and I straightened to reach his mouth better. I was in sky-high heels, but it wasn't quite enough to make up for our height difference. He kissed me with lots of lip and tongue, and I did the same back even though everyone was watching us.

Cane didn't seem to give a damn.

He finally broke away, giving me the most possessive look I'd ever seen. "Mrs. Barsetti."

I loved the name because it fit me like a glove. "What happened to Bellissima?"

"Bellissima Barsetti…suits you perfectly." He took my hand and guided me down the short aisle of our family. They threw white rose petals over us that drifted down and littered the grass.

My eyes were on the road ahead of us, the long future we had to enjoy.

But his eyes were on me——and only me.

Epilogue

CROW

"I'm so hideous."

"Are not." I moved on top of her, careful not to bump against her enormous belly. Button was nine months pregnant and ready to burst. She was uncomfortable, her back aching from the strain, and her feet hurting from the extra weight.

"Yes, I am." She pushed her hand against my chest. "There's no way you could possibly want to have sex with me."

"Then explain that." I nodded down to my crotch, where my fat cock was eager to be inside her.

When she couldn't explain it, she just stared at me. "I'm a cow."

"Shut up, Button. You're beautiful. Honestly, I'm gonna miss seeing you pregnant."

"Liar." At this final stage, she was argumentative and moody. She wasn't the calm and carefree woman I married. She was stressed, angry, and self-conscious. She never had low confidence about her body, but now she never wanted me to see her naked.

I shoved myself inside her, sliding through her slick pussy in an aggressive thrust.

That shut her right up. "God…"

I held myself higher off her body than usual so I wouldn't rub against her stomach. I stared at my wife's face as I fucked her the way I wanted. My arousal only increased with her pregnancy. I felt it was the most erotic thing I'd ever witnessed. I loved the swell of her breasts, the way her stomach kicked when the baby moved. I loved everything about it.

The second we started to move, she didn't have any more protests.

She fucked me as hard as I fucked her.

We moved, thrust, and grunted. Sweat poured down my back, and I loved every second of it. Within minutes, I made my beautiful wife scream my name with her orgasm. She wasn't thinking about how much her body had changed. She was just thinking about me.

And then I came, pumping her full.

Her head rolled back before she eyed me with an intense look of pleasure.

I kissed her then pulled out.

Like the heated moment hadn't happened, she covered herself with a sheet.

I had to stop myself from rolling my eyes.

She got out of bed then headed into the bathroom.

"You're being stupid. Did it seem like I didn't enjoy it?"

"Just leave me alone, Crow." She shut the door and shut me out.

I pulled my clothes on and brushed off her dismissal. Her moods had gotten progressively worse over the last month, so I was used to her attitude at this point. I liked her pregnant, but I didn't like her angry.

I stepped outside and came face-to-face with Lars.

"Cane is here to see you, sir. He's in the study."

"Thanks. I could use a drink." I walked across the hall and stepped inside.

Cane had helped himself to my scotch, always finding it no matter where I hid it. He held up his glass as I entered the room. "How's Pearl doing?"

"She's been better." I sat on the couch opposite him and made myself a drink. "She's angry, aggressive, self-conscious...you name it."

Cane chuckled. "Thankfully, Adelina hasn't gotten there yet. She's just sexy and pregnant. You know that glow people are always talking about? It's hot..." He drank from his glass then swirled the ice cubes around.

"Enjoy it while you can."

"Isn't Pearl due any day?"

"She's due any moment, actually," I said. "I can't wait until my son is here."

Cane smiled. "I can't believe you're having a boy. I wonder what I'm having."

"You guys could find out."

"She wants it to be a surprise for some reason..." He rolled his eyes. "Have you decided on a name?"

I finished my drink then poured another. "Conway Barsetti."

Cane smiled wider. "I like it. It's strong. It's different. But it reminds me of our names."

"They're extremely close."

"Pearl come up with that?"

"I did, actually."

"Conway." He said the name out loud slowly. "It's perfect. Are you getting nervous? It's one thing to talk about your son arriving, but it's another matter when they're here."

I had my doubts. I had my fears. But anything that came out of Button couldn't be scary. I'd have a son to raise into a man. I'd have someone to give my legacy to. If something happened to me, he'd be a man and look after his mother. That's how I would raise him to be, at least. Whatever I couldn't handle, Button would be there to help. "I think it'll be alright. Button will be a great mother."

"I'm sure. Adelina will too. God, I hope I don't have a girl." He rubbed his temple as he chuckled. "If a man even glances at her, I'd have to kill him."

"I know." The thought of having a girl didn't scare me. She'd be strong like Button. And she'd have a right hook like me.

"So, this is one of the last times it'll just be the two of us. First, the women came. And now, the kids are coming... Our lives have changed so much." He looked into the fire, his gold band reflecting the flames.

"Yeah...but I think they've changed in a good way."

"Crow!" Button's scream erupted in the house, shaking the walls and the foundation.

I dropped my glass, and it shattered on the floor.

Cane spilled his as he rushed to put it down.

I was on my feet and heading to the door, my heart pounding like a drum.

Button opened the door first, clutching her stomach in a loose dress. Her hair was still wet from the shower. "My water just broke."

Fuck, it was happening. I stared at her blankly for three seconds before I finally moved into action. "Alright, let's get you to the hospital." I took her by the hand and pulled her into the hallway.

"I can't believe he's coming." She walked with me, breathing hard. "He's coming."

"Cane?"

Cane jogged until he caught up to me. "Have Lars get the bags and meet us at the hospital. Got it?"

"I'm on it." Cane darted away.

"Alright, Button. It's time."

Instantly, she started crying. "I'm so sorry I've been so mean to you lately. I just—"

"You're carrying my son. You have the right to be as mean as you want. Forget about it."

"Crow…"

"I don't care, Button. All I care about is us meeting our son. Now let's go get him."

———

SEVERAL HOURS LATER, Conway Barsetti arrived.

He had my eyes. Her nose. My lips. Her hair.

A perfect blend of the two of us.

He was seven pounds of perfection, the most beautiful thing I'd ever seen. He fit in just a single palm because he was so small. I loved my wife with all my heart, and it was hard to believe I could love anything more than her.

But I did.

My son.

I stared at him for ten minutes, holding him in the crook of my arm while Button drifted off to sleep. It was just the two of us. He looked me in the eye, his blue-green eyes shaped exactly like mine. He seemed just as interested in me as I was in him.

I didn't view my father as a role model. He had a lot of issues, a lot of sins.

But I wanted it to be different with my own son. I wanted him to look up to me, to admire me, and to be proud of the Barsetti name. I wanted to protect him, to push him into becoming a man stronger than me. I wanted to teach him everything about the world, including the dark and twisted shit no one wanted to mention.

I wanted him to be prepared for the hatred, the fear, the terror.

So he could overcome it.

I was already proud of him for just sitting in my arms.

This was love in a whole new way.

The door cracked open, and Cane poked his head inside. He noticed Pearl was asleep, so he motioned with his hands to ask if he could come inside.

I nodded.

He and Adelina walked inside, her stomach round the way Pearl's had been six months ago. They took the seat beside me and tried to be quiet as they looked into my son's face.

"Aww..." Adelina covered her mouth as she gasped.

Cane grinned. "That's one handsome Barsetti."

I was already a proud father. "I know."

"He has your eyes," Cane said. "But he looks like Pearl too."

"He's so beautiful," Adelina whispered. "Congratulations."

"Thank you." Now I couldn't stop smiling.

Cane looked up at Pearl. "How's she doing?"

"She's exhausted," I said. "Four hours of hard labor. She saw Conway and then drifted off to sleep."

"I'm not looking forward to that part," Adelina whispered.

Cane moved his hand to her thigh. "You'll be great, *Bellissima*."

I hardly ever saw Cane without Adelina in tow. They were a pair, just the way Pearl and I were.

"Anything we can do for you?" Cane asked. "I was going to bring flowers, but you guys don't strike me as flower people."

"Because we aren't," I said with a laugh. "All we need right now is rest."

"You want us to watch the baby so you can take a nap?" Adelina asked.

The last thing I wanted to do was let go of Conway. "No...I'm wide awake."

———

BUTTON BREASTFED Conway for the first time in the hospital room. She was still in bed, but she'd showered and changed her gown. She got a full night of rest because I took care of Conway until he started crying at dawn.

I sat beside her and watched.

Conway latched on and started sucking.

"He already knows what he's doing," Pearl said with a chuckle.

I grinned. "He's just like me."

She chuckled then swatted my arm. "Conway will be a lot more sensitive than you."

"With a mother like you, I'm sure he will be."

Button seemed to forget I was there because she was too absorbed in looking at her son. She still looked radiant even though she was no longer pregnant. She still had a beautiful glow that surrounded her at all times. Her smile could light up an abandoned fireplace. "I got really uncomfortable at the end...but it was totally worth it."

"Yeah, it was."

She leaned down and kissed him on the forehead then returned to feeding him. She was a mother in love. I used to be the only recipient of that gaze, but now I'd been replaced.

It didn't bother me at all. "So, when do you want to make another one?"

She laughed as if I were joking.

"I'm being serious."

She looked up at me, the smile in her eyes. "I need at least a six-month break."

"I can wait. Then we're back at it."

"We haven't even taken this one home yet."

"Doesn't matter to me. Now that I've seen him, I know he's the greatest thing that ever happened to me."

Her eyes softened as she looked at me.

"As are you."

Epilogue II

Cane

Adelina started to waddle.

And damn, it was hot.

She shook her hips as she moved, her stomach wobbling from left to right. She was already sexy, but being pregnant just made her irresistible.

I couldn't keep my hands off her.

She sat beside me on the couch, her pregnant belly poking through her shirt.

My hand automatically moved to her distended stomach, hoping to feel movement underneath. The first time I felt my baby kick, I was over the moon. I couldn't think straight because I was blinded by joy. A year ago, the last thing I wanted was a wife and kids.

And now, I was so grateful I had both.

"My parents are coming over for dinner," she said. "Hope that's okay."

"I don't mind."

She pulled her hair into a ponytail and kept it off the back of her neck. It was a summer day, but the AC wasn't enough to keep her cool when she was carrying another person inside her.

"Want something to drink?"

"No. I'm just a little uncomfortable." She leaned back and rubbed her belly. "I still have three months to go. Pearl took it like a pro."

"Crow told me she was a nightmare."

"He did not."

"Okay, he didn't. But he did say she was difficult."

"Now I understand why." She moved closer into my side and rested her hand on my thigh. "How about we invite Pearl and Crow?"

"I'm sure they want to stay home with the baby."

"How will you know unless you ask?"

I grinned. "You got me there, Mrs. Barsetti."

———

We had dinner together on the terrace. The sun had just disappeared over the horizon, blanketing us with the cool breeze of evening. We dined on fresh baked bread, pasta Gerald made himself, Italy's finest wine—and with great company.

Adelina's parents took to Italy well. They didn't seem to miss the constant busyness of America. They loved the endless landscapes, the olive trees across the land, and the smell of wine and cheese everywhere they went.

And having them there made my wife very happy.

That made me happy.

Pearl held Conway most of the time, but she handed him off to Crow when she needed to use the restroom or eat. Now she was engaged in a conversation with Adelina's parents, a glass of wine in her hand for the first time in nearly a year.

That left Crow and me at the end, in our own little world.

I stared at him over my glass of wine, seeing him look happy without smiling. His son was cradled in a single arm, as if weightless. Conway was wrapped in a blue blanket, his eyes closed because he was asleep.

Crow looked over the horizon before his eyes drifted back to me. He noticed me staring at him, so he said, "What?"

"You look happy."

A slight smile stretched his lips.

"Our whole lives, you never looked happy. And now, you're happy all the time."

His eyes lit up, the usual darkness disappearing. "I don't think I knew what happiness was until recently."

"Yeah…"

He held my gaze. "And you look happy."

"Because I am."

"If you think you're happy now, wait until you meet your son or daughter for the first time. There's nothing like it."

My eyes glanced down to Conway. "Yeah...I can only imagine."

Epilogue III

Cane

Adelina's pregnancy wasn't as smooth as Pearl's.

The baby struggled during delivery, so they had to perform an emergency C-section.

I had to wait in the waiting room until they were finished.

And fuck, I was scared.

Crow was there beside me the whole time. He didn't feed me false words of comfort. His silence was all he could offer me, and I gladly took it.

Until the nurse brought me into the room.

And introduced me to my son.

I held him in my arms and felt his heaviness. He was only six pounds, but he felt dense. The weight of responsibility fell on my shoulders, and I suddenly held something priceless in my hands. It was more important than all of my assets.

It was my family.

I turned to Adelina, who was covered in sweat and tears. "*Bellissima*, are you alright?"

"I'm okay," she whispered. "It was just scary there for a second. But we're both alright."

I cradled my son and kissed her on the forehead.

"We need a name," she whispered. "We've been arguing for a while, but we need to decide."

I hadn't known if we were having a boy or girl, not like Crow did. This was a surprise for both of us because she'd wanted it that way. But at the same time, I wasn't surprised at all. It seemed like I'd always known what would come out of her. "Carter?" Now that I'd met him, seen him with my own eyes, I felt like I knew him.

Adelina nodded. "Yes…Carter."

I sat at the bedside with him in my arms. I spent all my time taking care of my wife, but now I had to make room for one more person. But with someone so small, it shouldn't be a problem, not when my heart was so big. "Thank you, *Bellissima*."

"For what?" she asked.

"Giving me my boy." I brought him to my lips and kissed his forehead. "I'm a dad…it's weird."

"It's not weird," she whispered. "It's right."

"Yeah…" I felt like I was hogging him, so I transferred him back to her arms. "You did all the work. Your turn."

She smiled and cradled him to her chest. "He's perfect. I couldn't have asked for a more beautiful baby."

"No, you couldn't."

"Carter and Conway...they'll be the best of friends."

"I'm sure they will be." I pictured them playing together the way Crow and I did. Our children would have their own siblings, but I knew our kids would always be close. We lived five miles apart, and we would always live five miles apart from each other. "Your parents are here. They're eager to see the baby."

"I know." She stared down at Carter. "But I want it to be just the three of us for a little longer."

We sat in silence together, admiring the little man we made together. I never would have imagined my life like this. Five years ago, I was a criminal who killed without thinking. All I cared about was money and power. But now, I didn't think about the business that I gave to Constantine. I didn't think about making money. I didn't care about any of those things. All I really cared about was my family—and not just the three of us.

Crow and I had both turned our backs on our legacy. We could have followed in our father's footsteps, but we took our own path. We made our own lives while honoring the Barsetti name. Now we were surrounded by our wives and children. Life would pass quickly, but we would enjoy it so thoroughly.

How did I get so lucky?

Adelina turned back to me, knowing my mind had drifted. "What?"

I smiled at her, watching the love of my life hold my son. "Nothing...nothing at all."

Thank You!

Thanks so much for sticking with Crow, Cane, and Pearl through this incredible adventure. They aren't just characters to me but real people that I adore. When I'm making a cup of coffee in the morning, sometimes I wonder, "What are the Barsetti Brothers doing today? Working at the winery?"

I have a new series in mind that I'm excited to share with you. Once it's available, you'll be the first to know! I know it's hard to accept the end of the Buttons Series. I admit, I cried when I wrote the last ten pages of this story. But your encouragement kept me going.

Thanks again for being an awesome fan. Your support means the world to me.

XOXO,

Thank You!

Pene

Made in the USA
Columbia, SC
21 December 2017